PORTRAIT OF ADRIAN

Jackie Arnold and Jonathan Nelson had been friends for years. Jackie realised that she was in love with Jon but didn't want to be rushed into anything serious and she wasn't sure that Jon felt the same way about her. So when she received an invitation to stay with her two aunts in Devon, it was an opportunity for Jackie and Jonathan to sort out their feelings. But then Jackie met Adrian Naismith, good-looking and obviously interested in her. Was he going to make her forget Jon?

MARY CUMMINS

PORTRAIT OF ADRIAN

Complete and Unabridged

LINFORD
Leicester

First published in Great Britain in 1973

First Linford Edition
published 2006

All the characters in this book have no existence
outside the imagination of the Author, and have no
relation whatsoever to anyone bearing the same name
or names. They are not even distantly inspired by any
individual known or unknown to the Author, and all
the incidents are pure invention

British Library CIP Data

Cummins, Mary
    Portrait of Adrian.—Large print ed.—
Linford romance library
1. Love stories
2. Large type books
I. Title
823.9'14 [F]

ISBN 1–84617–181–4

Published by
F. A. Thorpe (Publishing)
Anstey, Leicestershire

Set by Words & Graphics Ltd.
Anstey, Leicestershire
Printed and bound in Great Britain by
T. J. International Ltd., Padstow, Cornwall

This book is printed on acid-free paper

1

It was a lovely warm morning in early June. Jackie Arnold threw open the bedroom window at Garth Cottage and gazed down at a bed of roses, freshly into bloom and filling the soft air with perfume. She had dreamed of this moment towards the final term at art college in London, and now that she *was* home, and was putting the finishing touches to her first commission, she ought to have been feeling completely happy.

Yet is one ever completely happy for long? wondered Jackie, as she withdrew her head, and began to tidy up after finishing the varnishing of her picture. It was of nearby Chipping Sodbury, bathed in sunshine, and especially beautiful because it had been painted with love.

Brigadier Nelson at Merton Lodge

loved the place, and commissioned Jackie to paint it, knowing that she loved it, too. The finished picture gave her cause for satisfaction, but there was a strange anti-climax about it all, and with the finish of this piece of work, she must now inevitably ask the question, what now?

Jackie had been born in Garth Cottage which had belonged to her mother's people, but she had spent her twenty-two years between Chipping Sodbury and London. Her father, Richard Arnold, had been a stock-broker, but when he died, two years ago, her mother had decided that she wanted to live at the cottage perma-nently, after a small prod from Jackie.

Their flat in London had been sold, and Jackie found new lodgings while she was at college, but she had lived for the day when she would finish her training and come home to join her mother at the cottage.

Janet Arnold had been shaken by the death of her husband, realising how much she had leaned on him over the years. She saw, gradually, that she had been living Richard's life, not her own, and it was as though she did not know herself any more. Her own tastes and talents had been submerged so that she could share everything with him, and when he died she began to realise that the friends they had made weren't really her friends, and that the orchestral concerts and operas which she had enjoyed with Richard weren't really her kind of music at all.

Even the flat was dull and sombre, with only a few of the frills which she loved. Yet she could not remember what she had been like before she had fallen in love with Richard. The Janet Hamilton of those days hadn't been much of a personality in her own eyes, and she had quickly adapted to what her husband expected of her. After twenty-five years of marriage, Janet Arnold could no longer remember much about Janet Hamilton.

Jackie had worried about her, even

though she was kept busy with her work at art college.

'Can't you go out a little more, Mother? You're . . . ' She looked at her mother's small slender figure. 'You're losing weight.'

'Most of my friends spend their lives trying to lose weight,' she laughed. 'You aren't exactly plump yourself.'

Jackie grinned. She had her mother's long honey-gold hair and dark blue eyes, but she was bigger boned, like her father, and looked lithe and vigorous.

'No, but I look disgustingly healthy. Mother, why aren't you going home to the cottage? You know that's what you want to do. Is it because of me?'

Mrs Arnold coloured. She *had* been thinking that it was the only way she could find herself again. Back in Chipping Sodbury, where she had been brought up, remembering all the things she had loved to do as a girl, she might find herself again. Yet she couldn't leave Jackie in London by herself!

'But you need the flat, darling,' she

protested. 'You know I can't.'

'Why not?' asked Jackie. 'It's what you want, isn't it?'

Her mother nodded, then agreed happily.

Garth Cottage was a pretty place, and after a few weeks of listlessness, Janet had begun to look at her old home and remember how nicely her mother had kept it, with white frilled curtains, pot plants, lots of ornaments and the garden ablaze with flowers.

Over the years, as they had all used the cottage, Richard's more ascetic taste had asserted itself, and cupboards bulged with things which had been put away. Janet enjoyed herself bringing them all out again.

The garden had flourished under her skilful fingers — how she had missed it at the flat! — and as she found her own friends locally and felt secure and happy in the background which was entirely her own, she had blossomed out into a new Janet Arnold.

At first Jackie had welcomed the

change and loved it. The cottage was surely everyone's dream come true, she thought, looking round at all its fresh daintiness. And her mother looked years younger!

Coming down from College, Jackie had thrown herself on to their old chintz-covered settee and stretched luxuriously.

'Just think,' she said. 'No more rush hour, crowded tubes, scrambling about for food and being deafened by noise. If I can't work here, Mother, where can I work?'

'Isn't it wonderful that you *can* work at home?' said Janet. 'You might have wanted to be a secretary, or something, where you had to live in the city. But now you can just keep on painting your pictures . . . Oh, I've got the smallest bedroom prepared for you, as a studio, I mean. I've cleared it all out, and you can use it as you wish. I . . . I thought it would spare your bedroom . . . '

It was the first tiny discord. Jackie had dashed upstairs to look, then came down rather more slowly.

'Sorry, Mother, it's no use,' she said gently. 'There just isn't enough light. No, I'll have to use my bedroom, I'm afraid. It's the only one bright enough.'

'But, darling, I bought such a pretty carpet. And your bedspread! I mean, you do tend to get paint on things.'

'I'll be careful,' Jackie promised. 'I can spread down papers and things. We can put down an old carpet at the window, and a table for all my stuff.'

'All right,' agreed Mrs Arnold doubt-fully.

There was no doubt that the mechanics of painting made a rather jarring note in the home.

'Always supposing I can sell my work,' went on Jackie, though perhaps there was no desperate hurry about that. It had struck her now and again that she had no real idea how they stood financially, but they had always been very comfortable and no doubt her father had ensured that it would always be so.

But now her mother was looking a trifle embarrassed again, and Jackie always liked to know how she stood.

'You and Daddy were always very generous,' she said bluntly, 'and I know I've got a small nest egg which Granny Hamilton left for me, but how are we fixed now, Mother? Do I need to earn a good living, and help you with finances?'

'Not quite as bad as that, dear,' said Janet hastily. 'I can manage just ordinary expenses, but you'll have to do your bit, Jackie. The cost of living, you know . . . and I have spent rather a lot here. And your father's income did go up and down, though he had provided for us, of course. We'll go into it properly, my dear.'

They did, and Jackie felt better when she knew the position more clearly. In fact, it was exhilarating to realise she would have to stand on her own feet and contribute towards the upkeep of their home. She would need to earn her living.

Then it was frightening. In the dreams she'd had before leaving college, she had given herself time to paint lots of pictures, then she'd had an exhibition where she had sold everything quite easily, and had people coming to her for more. But now there was no time, and the dreams had been just dreams.

Should she try for a teaching post? she wondered, then put that behind her. That raised further difficulties, and she just wasn't a teacher. Should she do some quick oil sketches, and ask a kind shopkeeper to display them for her?

Jackie had gone for a walk to think it out, and was startled when a sleek dark blue car stopped beside her, and Jonathan Nelson poked out his head. She had known Jon most of her life, when the Nelsons lived in Chipping Sodbury.

But now Brigadier Nelson, his wife and son, had moved about fifteen miles away to Merton Lodge, when the Brigadier's mother died, and Jackie hadn't seen quite so much of Jon in recent years.

He looked just the same, she thought, going over to the car, then revised that first impression. Jon's face was still fresh, with the curly brown hair any girl might envy, but his face was leaner and there were new lines about his mouth.

'Just been to the cottage,' he told her. 'Your mother said you'd come this way. Hop in and we'll go home for tea.'

Jackie lost no time. They often had people dropping in for tea, but they were mainly her mother's friends. It would be much more fun to have Jonathan. She'd thought about him often in recent months, but had to admit that he was the most attractive man she knew. If she had been a romantic, she might have fancied herself in love with him, but her heart was untouched, even though she was often very glad that he hadn't gone off and married someone else!

'This is nice, Jon,' she said, climbing

into the car. 'I was just thinking about you the other day. Finished at university now? I know you're a couple of years ahead of me, but architecture takes longer.'

'Yes. I'm doing practical again in an office in Bath, but I wanted to know what you were doing. I never see enough of you. Usually I get on the telephone to the cottage in time to hear that you've disappeared back to London, or that you're sunning yourself in Torquay.'

'Not this time, Jon,' she laughed. 'I'm home for good, though . . . ' her eyes sobered, ' . . . I'll have to make my way now, and that isn't going to be easy. Still, no doubt I'll get a start some-where. I can't even go and help the aunts . . . '

'The aunts?'

'Yes. You know . . . Aunt Maude and Aunt Hetty, Daddy's two sisters. They used to run a boarding house in Torquay, and allow me to tell you that when I went there, I wasn't sunning myself. I was helping them as a holiday job, so there! Only now they've retired and have bought a little house near Goodrington instead.'

She realised she was chattering, and stopped. Yet she had felt oddly nervous of Jonathan Nelson. He looked rather different from the rather gangling boy he had been, and there was a new air of authority about him.

'Good for them,' he said, slowing down for a bend.

'Jon!' she cried, 'this isn't the way home. I've been so busy talking I didn't notice.'

'I meant *my* home, of course,' he told her briefly. 'I told your mother.'

'But, Jon, I can't go to your home for tea, looking like this! I've only got on my old jeans and jersey.'

This time he grinned and looked much more like himself.

'How like a woman! I thought the artist in you wouldn't care. You're clean, aren't you? Not likely to soil the chairs by any chance?'

'Heavens, no!'

'There you are, then.' His voice changed, growing rather more serious. 'You look fine to me, Jacqueline, whatever you wear. I tell you that for what it's worth.'

She found herself colouring, and said nothing, not sure what to reply.

'Anyway, there's only Mother and Father at home. And Mother's been gardening.'

The car was powerful and they arrived at Merton Lodge in no time. It had always pleased Jackie to come here. There was something which satisfied her to see the solid iron gates of the old house, and the long winding drive.

For a while there had been a slight air of neglect about the place which had saddened her a little. The old house had looked in need of a coat of paint and some small repairs, and the creepers had been allowed to run riot, but today Jackie was happy to see it beginning to look cared for again.

'How nice the Lodge looks,' she

remarked to Jonathan as the car swung over the gravel to the front of the house, which was solid Georgian. 'Not that it hasn't *always* looked nice,' she added hastily, and Jonathan grinned.

'Now you've given yourself away. You thought it was a mess for a while. Well, it was!'

For a moment the grim look was back round his mouth, and he looked older and rather hard. Again Jackie had the strange feeling of unfamiliarity, thinking how little she really knew Jon Nelson. They had gone dancing together, played tennis, and she had thought of him rather casually, as one does with a boy one has known for years. But now she realised, almost with a sense of shock, that she didn't really know him at all. She didn't know what he was thinking or how he felt about various things, but she could imagine how his eyebrows would shoot up if she suddenly asked for his views on the political state of the country.

Now he was frowning up at the house

as he helped her out of the car, and she could not even guess whether he loved or hated it. Perhaps he had been happier in their smaller house, near Chipping Sodbury, but after old Mrs Nelson died, the Brigadier had decided to move to the Lodge which had been his since the death of his father, and which would be Jonathan's one day.

'There's plenty of ground to look after,' she remarked, thinking of their small pretty garden at Garth Cottage.

'Yes,' agreed Jonathan, almost curtly, and she felt rebuffed. Then he smiled again, and took her hand, leading her up the steps and through the front door.

'Mother! Father!' he called, almost gaily. 'A visitor for tea.'

A door opened to the left of the hall, and Mrs Nelson hurried out. She was tall and elegant, even in a rather shapeless slatey-blue dress, but she smiled warmly when she saw Jacqueline, as did the Brigadier, when he followed her out of the room.

'Jacqueline, my dear! We heard you were home. I saw Constance Naylor in Bath last week. I've been meaning to call on your mother, but the decorators are in the drawing room. It's such a nuisance. So inconvenient.'

'But so necessary,' put in Jonathan, a glint in his eyes.

'I liked it as it was,' complained Brigadier Nelson. 'Got used to it . . . '

'Over the years,' finished Jonathan. 'We know. But that's just it, Father. It's been *years* since it was touched, and it's high time we did the place up.'

'So you keep telling us. Change, change, change all the time with you young people. Nothing's any good unless it's new.'

'Now that's not my view, Father,' said Jonathan, then stopped rather suddenly, looking at his mother, then Jackie. 'Sorry. Am I getting into another argument? We've come for tea, haven't we, Jackie? Not a lecture. Are we in time?'

'Of course. I'm just setting the

trolley. Mrs Whiteley has gone home now.'

'Then I'll help,' offered Jackie. 'It's too bad of me to descend on you like this.'

'Now it's you who is talking non-sense, my dear. Yes, you can help, and you, Jon, can lift out that small table and Bruce can look for some paper napkins to save washing, even if they *do* slide off your knee, dear.'

Evelyn Nelson was pleased to see Jacqueline. She had watched the girl grow up, and she had known Janet Arnold since they were girls together. If Jonathan would only settle for a girl like Jackie, then she and the Brigadier would be more than happy. In fact, she had thought it would all be arranged that way. Jonathan had always been an easy-going boy and more than willing to be guided by his parents.

But in recent years, months almost, he had become much more difficult to manage, especially since moving to the Lodge. He and Bruce were often at

17

loggerheads over the place, and instead of recognising his father's authority, Jonathan's chin had stuck out aggressively and Bruce had found himself giving way over quite a few points.

'Getting on his feet, and being made to feel independent now that . . . well, you know what I mean, dear . . . has turned his head,' Bruce had complained. 'Some of the buildings he designed while doing his 'sandwich' year are already going up and it's done something to him. We'll have to handle him rather more carefully, Evelyn.'

'He should marry a nice girl and settle down,' Mrs Nelson had decided practically. 'Jacqueline Arnold, for instance.'

'I agree,' the Brigadier told her, 'but if we as much as hint at the idea, he'll avoid the girl like the plague. Just to be different!'

'You could be right,' mused Mrs Nelson, 'but I think he's attracted to Jackie.'

'He's turned out too hard-headed for

anything like that,' growled his father, sore because the dining-room was next on Jonathan's list. But just let him touch his den! He'd probably end up with upheaval over the whole house, but if Jon laid one finger on his old room, he would have to teach the boy a lesson.

So now Jacqueline was welcomed warmly, but not quite so effusively as she might, and she could sense a certain amount of tension in the air. Was it from the family? Or was it herself? She hoped they didn't think she was chasing Jonathan!

'And what are you doing now, dear?' Mrs Nelson was asking. 'Do you go to work on a magazine or something?'

'No, I'm afraid I paint pictures,' said Jackie, 'such as landscapes or seascapes. I think those are my best efforts.'

'Not portraits?' asked the Brigadier.

'I *can* do portraits, and have done one or two of Mummy, though I don't think she likes them much!'

'I'd like to have a look at those,' said

Jonathan, lighting his pipe. 'Was it head and shoulders?'

'No, I rather sketched her while she was down grubbing away in the flower beds.'

'Oh, that explains it,' laughed Mrs Nelson. 'I wouldn't like anyone to paint *me* in my old hat and gardening gloves!'

'You're making a nice job of looking after it, though,' said Jackie, and there was a silence.

'Well . . . ' began the Brigadier.

'I've attended to it,' said Jon briefly. 'As you say, Jackie, it is looking better.'

'So what will you do?' Mrs Nelson asked again, rather hurriedly. 'Do you just paint pictures, then try to sell them?'

'Something like that. Or I might get a commission to paint something special.'

'I'll give you one,' said the Brigadier, and they all looked at him, rather astonished. If there was one thing at Merton Lodge which was fairly plentiful, it was pictures. Jackie had often wandered round looking at them, but apart from one or two which were really outstanding, they weren't really very good. Previous Nelsons seemed to have bought with a view to covering the walls rather than with care and discrimination.

'One what?' asked Jackie.

'One commission. To paint me a picture of Chipping Sodbury. The High Street, with the sun shining on it. Now that would make a picture, wouldn't it?'

Jackie knew how much the Brigadier loved the place, and she felt her own enthusiasm stirring.

'It can grace our new drawing room,' the Brigadier went on. 'What do you say, my dear?'

'A splendid idea,' said Mrs Nelson. 'Don't you think so, Jon?'

'Can you afford to pay Jackie's prices?' asked Jon, and she flushed, but not so red as Brigadier Nelson.

'Now look here, young Jon, you're going too far!' he began.

'It's all right!' cried Jackie. 'I shall love doing it, and just for this time . . .'

'You start as you mean to go on,' finished Jon. 'I wonder if anyone appreciates the skill, time, and care, not to mention mere materials which goes into making a picture. Suppose it took a couple of months. Six pictures per year. What sort of money would you expect her to earn?'

'She can put her own price on it, and I shall be happy to buy it,' said his father.

'You hear that, Jackie? You've got a commission. Name your own price.'

Then Jon laughed, his voice full of gaiety again, and the atmosphere lightened.

'All right,' she agreed, caught by his mood, 'though I shan't take two months. I'll bring it over as soon as it's finished, and varnished. What about framing?'

'I'll attend to that,' said Jon. 'It had better fit in with the pictures we intend to re-hang.'

'And that's all of them,' insisted the Brigadier.

'Then we'll have to nail Jackie's to the ceiling,' retorted his son, and somehow they were all laughing again.

But as she said goodbye to the Nelsons, with an invitation ringing in her ears to come back again soon, Jackie's eyes were a trifle puzzled. Was Jonathan, too, finding it a little bit difficult to settle down at home after being away? Was he inflicting his own tastes on his parents?

They were both rather quiet on the journey home, and at Garth Cottage Jon helped her out of the car, then smoothed back her lovely pale golden hair with a rather touching gesture, which made her heart leap.

'Now that you're home, Jackie,' he said quietly, 'I hope we can talk again some time. Good luck with the picture.'

He hopped into the car and drove away at his usual speed, and she was left feeling rather shaken. It had been a strange day, and a disturbing visit to Merton Lodge. She could feel changes somewhere, either in the Nelsons, in

Jonathan, or in herself. Her return home had not brought the placid halcyon days she had expected.

But she had a commission! Her first! Suddenly joy in her work filled her heart, and she almost ran indoors to find her mother.

'I'm painting Chipping Sodbury . . . High Street . . . for the Brigadier,' she said breathlessly. 'Isn't that wonderful?'

'Wonderful,' agreed Mrs Arnold happily. 'Good for you, darling. You're launched.'

Jackie hoped she would stay launched! And afloat!

2

It had been fun doing the picture, though there had been more work in it than she had supposed, and she knew that the fee she had arranged with the Brigadier would hardly give her much profit after the cost of materials had been deducted. She was not likely to get fat on her earnings, to begin with at any rate, even if she was kept constantly in work.

Jonathan called to see her while she was working on the picture.

'I'm going over to Barwell Green . . . you know that place about six miles from here?'

She nodded. She should know it! They had often gone on picnics nearby, as youngsters.

'There's a barn which is going to be converted, and I've been asked to submit plans. I thought we could mix a little pleasure with work.'

'It will still be work for you,' said Jackie, 'but what about me? I'd have to leave mine!'

Jon looked disconcerted.

'I'm sorry, I forgot.'

Jackie grinned mischievously.

'People do tend to forget that painting pictures is work,' she agreed, 'but I'll let you off this time, especially since it's your father who will be kept waiting.'

'He won't mind,' Jonathan told her. 'He's got into a state where he hates change. The Lodge . . . ' He broke off, then grinned again. 'We won't discuss the Lodge. That's between him and me.'

'Perhaps . . . perhaps it isn't a good thing to force older people to make changes,' put in Jackie.

The grim look was back on his face.

'It could be necessary.'

Jackie looked at him uneasily. Jon seemed to be growing so hard, and she could not help remembering a conversation she'd had with her mother after her last visit to the Lodge.

'Jon seems to be making heaps of improvements,' she'd commented, 'though I don't think the Brig likes being disturbed. No doubt they'll be glad of it all, though, when Jon's finished with it. That's what comes of choosing architecture.'

'Just so long as they can afford it,' her mother said lightly. 'I don't think there was much money left when old Mrs Arnold died, and pensions aren't exactly enormous these days.'

'No,' agreed Jackie thoughtfully.

Surely Jon could not be forcing his father to have all these improvements when he could not afford them. Yet the Brigadier had seemed relieved when she had put a modest fee on her picture, and he had always been a generous person.

But Jonathan was smiling at her, his dark eyes gleaming.

'Surely you know me well enough to trust me not to lock you up in the barn, or have you walk home. I've even put some goodies in a basket.'

'Oh, Jon!' she protested, laughing. 'Give me five minutes to get the paint off, and change out of these old jeans.'

'All right. Five minutes.'

Her five minutes was more than doubled by the time she came to join her mother and Jon in the kitchen. She looked elegant and charming in a lavender suit, her pale gold hair gleaming.

'Don't worry if we're a little late,' Jon said to Janet Arnold. 'I'll try to persuade her to relax a little this evening, in Bristol, or we may go out to dinner somewhere.'

'I haven't said I'd go,' said Jackie.

'I haven't asked you yet,' returned Jonathan, and smiled at her mother. 'I'll see her safely home either by teatime or bedtime, according to her wishes.'

'And yours, I suppose,' said Mrs Arnold.

She watched them go, wondering a little about Jonathan. She hoped Jackie was not falling in love with him.

Janet thought about her own marriage, and how she had had to submerge her own personality for the sake of giving Richard all the love and comfort she felt he needed. Now she wondered if that had been a mistake. She would want someone just right for Jackie. Yet what sort of man would be right for Jackie? It would have to be someone dependable, yet someone who would not bore her either.

Janet sighed. It was times like these when she missed Richard. He had always taken any problems on to his own shoulders, and had not allowed her to worry. Now she had her own sort of freedom, but there were worries attached to it as well.

For Jackie it was a day to remember. Jonathan was much more like the happy boy she had known over the years. She watched him with interest when they reached Barwell Green, as he became the competent architect, making notes and taking measurements, while he surveyed the whole area as though he were getting the feel of the place.

After a time Jackie left him to his work, and began to sort out the picnic he had brought, but it was some time before Jon returned, then he apologised for leaving her.

'Have you eaten everything?' he asked. 'If so, it would serve me right, and I'm ravenous.'

'Eaten everything! I like that! I haven't even touched a bun.'

'Let's tuck in, Jackie darling, then I suggest we head for Bristol. What about seeing a film for a change, then we can have a proper meal and I'll take you home.'

Her cheeks had coloured at the endearment. Jonathan Nelson wasn't the man to scatter them about, and she wondered if he meant it. Was she still just the youthful companion to him, or had she become more important?

They were quiet. But then they were often quiet in one another's company. It had always been one of the things she liked about Jon. She could just relax and be herself, and dream a little without feeling obliged to keep him entertained. And he, too, was often quiet when he chose.

But now she felt uncomfortably aware of him as they sat sharing out sandwiches. He had never even kissed her properly, she thought, and wondered if it had also crossed his mind as he glanced at her from time to time.

'I don't think I want to go to Bristol, Jon,' she said at length. Her nerves were beginning to jangle a little, and somehow she would have to know where she stood with Jon before spending so much time in his company. Already she could feel a slight air of tension between them.

He gazed at her, his eyes dark.

'No?'

'No. I . . . I'm like you. I have work to do. If I leave a picture for very long, I go off it, and can't finish it properly.'

'I shouldn't have dragged you away.'

'No.'

This wasn't what she had meant to say, and somehow the day was beginning to go wrong, but she didn't know how to put things right.

Now it was Jonathan Nelson, the stranger, who was beside her again and he was laughing a little as he gathered up the picnic things, though not the joyous, happy laughter of earlier.

'Sorry, Jackie. I did rather bulldoze you, didn't I? Come on and I'll deliver you off in time for tea.'

Unhappily she climbed back into the car, feeling an almost unbearable disappointment. What was wrong with her? she wondered. Why ask him to take her home when she would have enjoyed a night out so much?

If only she understood Jonathan a bit better. But she was beginning to feel she didn't understand him at all. Or herself either, come to that.

★ ★ ★

'I feel like celebrating,' said Jackie, when the picture was finished. 'What do you think of it, Mother?'

'It's lovely, darling. Brigadier Nelson *will* be pleased.'

'Yes . . . well . . . '

It was no use asking Mother for criticism, she thought, though she felt in her bones that she could well be satisfied with her work.

The past week had been irksome, and she had thought a great deal about Jonathan. He had not called or rung her again, and she wondered if he had taken her refusal to go out with him to mean that she just was not interested.

She had begun to find the cottage rather stifling, too. The rooms were small and cosy compared to their home in London, and she had a lot of her father in her, preferring room to breathe and lack of fuss. She had gone for a few walks by herself, her hands deep in the pockets of her duffle coat, thinking about the future and wondering just where the right path lay.

A letter had come from the aunts at Goodrington, and Mrs Arnold read it with a smile. For years they had run a boarding house at Babbacombe, but in March of this year they had decided it was time to retire, and had bought a small house near Goodrington.

'Not a bungalow, dear,' Maude Arnold had written, 'but a house. Hetty and I would not like to sleep so near the ground, since we were used to the attics.'

Every year since starting college, Jackie had spent part of her summer vacation helping the aunts as a holiday job. She had enjoyed this very much, and it had been a small bone of contention between her and her mother, who thought that the aunts were on to a good thing.

But Jackie had respected Aunt Maude's point of view, that she had to do a good day's work for her salary, and time off to roam around Torbay, which she loved.

When the letter came, Jackie realised

how much she had missed it all this year, but wisely she kept that to herself, knowing that her mother would be hurt.

'They don't seem to be settling down *too* well, do they?' asked Janet, as she read the letter aloud. 'They're inviting us both down to see the new house, but I don't really feel I want to go at the moment. I've promised to help out at quite a few local functions, and I suppose you're busy with the picture.'

Jackie nodded, and took the letter to read it for herself. It was not quite like Aunt Maude's usual flowing style, and she said little about her sister. Could it be that they'd had a small quarrel? she wondered. Yet one thing she had liked about both had been their ability to get on with one another. They had each had their job to do at the boarding house. Maude had looked after the business end while Hetty had attended to the practical side, which assured comfort for their guests. Jackie had always thought they managed their boarding house competently and gave good value for money.

But now there was an odd sort of reticence about their letter, though they urged her to pay them a visit, and Janet, too, of course, though Jackie had always got on better with the aunts than Janet. The business streak in them had always repelled her.

Jackie had written back to say she had a commission at the moment, but she would write again when her picture was finished.

And now it was all ready and drying out, though she would advise them to leave it for some weeks yet before being framed like the other pictures, some of which Jackie envied him very much, standing out like jewels amongst the poorer ones.

'He's got one or two signed proofs by Russell Flint, and there's a small oil painting which I should like to see again after cleaning,' she had told Jonathan after her last visit.

'I'll see to it,' he promised her.

'Along with everything else?'

She had meant to tease him, but his face was serious and his eyes rather cool.

'Certainly. Along with everything else.'

Jackie rang up Merton Lodge, feeling oddly nervous. She wondered if she should ask for Jonathan, but when Mrs Nelson answered the telephone, she merely told her the picture was now finished.

'Oh, splendid,' said Mrs Nelson. 'I'll tell Bruce straight away. What about bringing it over? Could you do that, dear?'

'Oh yes. Mother and I have a small yellow Mini . . . '

'Of course you have. I forgot. I only asked because it would be rather nice if you could both come to dinner on Saturday evening, and bring the picture with you. Would you ask your mother, Jackie dear?'

Jackie put down the telephone and went to find her mother in the garden.

'What about it?' she asked. 'Dinner at the Lodge on Saturday when we take the picture.'

'Oh, good. That will be nice. Say yes, darling.'

Jackie's eyes shone with anticipation as she put down the telephone. Suddenly things were going right again and she looked forward to Saturday. Perhaps she could even run to a new dress, if her mother felt like popping into Bristol for an hour.

'Let's celebrate after all,' said Janet, 'just the two of us before we part with the picture. You can get a new dress, Jackie, then we can go and see a film or something, then have a meal.'

It was much the same sort of programme that Jonathan had suggested, and for a moment Jackie's cheeks flushed, then she put all that foolishness behind her. She had been getting herself into an odd sort of state over Jon. From now on she would be just the same good friend she had always been, and she would be a willing companion if he wanted to take her out again.

They had a quick lunch, then Jackie drove them both into Bristol in the small Mini, and they spent a happy afternoon shopping, then relaxed as they watched a film. It was Janet's first visit to a cinema since she had left London and she found herself enjoying it very much.

'I'm starving,' she announced as they came out of the cinema. 'Let's have a proper meal in one of the hotels. Which one, I wonder?'

Jackie remembered having a meal in Bristol with Jon once before, and she took her mother's arm.

'This way, then. I know somewhere nice.'

The dining room of the hotel was comfortable and fairly busy, but a small table was found for two, and Janet looked round, feeling that she was enjoying herself. She and Richard had often had dinner out, but she had dropped the habit at the cottage, feeling she could not go alone. But now it was fun with Jackie beside her.

Then she saw Jackie stiffen a little, and the warm blood leave her cheeks, then colour them again rosily. Janet glanced over to where Jackie was staring, and saw Jonathan Nelson with a very beautiful girl whose dark hair was swept back, showing the perfect oval of her face.

'It's Jonathan,' said Jackie hurriedly. 'Mummy, do you think we ought to go?'

'Go?' asked Janet. 'But . . . but the waiter is just coming with our order . . .'

'Of course.'

Jackie had obviously taken hold of herself.

'Silly of me,' she said hurriedly. 'I . . . just didn't want to embarrass him, that's all. That . . . that's probably his girl-friend.'

Janet had also felt a sense of shock, though not at seeing Jonathan. It was at Jackie's reaction to him sitting nearby with another girl. She had hoped Jackie was not falling in love with Jonathan, but now she could see that her hopes had come to nothing. It was now obvious why she had bought the new dress, and why she had been so excited at the prospect of delivering the picture, and having dinner at the Lodge.

Yet almost in a moment Jackie had hold of herself again, and her mother felt pride and admiration warm her heart, even as she felt saddened by it all. Janet did not know how things stood between Jackie and Jonathan, but she could see the proud tilt to her daughter's head, as Jonathan rose and came over to greet them, then introduce his companion as a friend of his, Janetta Hodge.

'How do you do, Miss Hodge,' said Jackie clearly, and smiled.

'Shall we ask the waiter to join our tables?' asked Jonathan.

'Oh no, please. It's lovely to see you both, but Mother and I have just come for a quick meal before going home. We don't want to trouble you.'

Miss Hodge looked relieved, and after a moment Jon gave a small nod.

'Very well. Though I hope to see you both on Saturday. I understand the picture is finished now.'

'Yes.'

'It's lovely,' put in Janet. 'I'm sure you'll like it.'

'It's my father's picture,' said Jonathan politely, and again there was an awkward silence, though it was Jackie who smoothed it over.

'You'll want to finish dinner,' she smiled. 'Don't let us keep you, Jon. Goodbye, Miss Hodge. Have a nice evening.'

'We usually do,' said Janetta Hodge sweetly. 'Don't we, Jon?'

'Of course,' he agreed.

Carefully Jackie avoided looking too closely at her mother for the rest of the meal, though she sat back looking as though she was enjoying her night out. On the way home they talked of general things, then Jackie decided she was tired and would go straight to bed.

Lying in bed, she looked at the ceiling, her heart churning away leadenly. It had been a shock to see Jon with another girl, but she realised he must surely go out with other people. He had probably invited out dozens of girls . . . or was it only the one? Was Janetta Hodge someone special? She had rather hinted that they often went out together, and she was certainly a very beautiful girl.

But Jackie still felt a sense of shock, though it wasn't entirely at seeing Jonathan with Janetta Hodge. It was at her own reaction. Because something seemed to have stabbed her to the heart. She had wondered how she felt about Jonathan Nelson, and now she knew. She was deeply in love with him, and even now the unfamiliar taste of jealousy was in her mouth.

But obviously he did not feel the same way about her. He must still think of her as his childhood companion, someone not even as close as a sister.

Some sort of cousin, perhaps.

Slow tears gathered and ran down her cheeks. She had looked forward to coming home for so long, but now she wished heartily that her course had not finished. If only she had been returning to London soon!

The new dress was now hanging in her wardrobe, but now it was only a dress, and not something new and exciting for Saturday.

Jackie buried her head in the pillows and longed for sleep, and it was a long time before she slept through sheer exhaustion. With great understanding, Janet allowed her to sleep late the following morning, and seemed not to notice the puffy look round Jackie's eyes.

So Jackie *had* been hurt. Yet perhaps it was just as well. Jonathan Nelson seemed to have grown into a very forceful young man. She was not sure he had enough understanding for Jackie!

★ ★ ★

On Saturday Jackie still found satisfaction in wearing her new dress, a pale silvery turquoise which brought out the gold in her hair. Her mother looked very chic in a dress of sapphire blue.

'We both look very grand, don't we?' she laughed. 'We should have kept your father's old Bentley.'

'Well, it is an occasion,' said Jackie.

'Unveiling your first picture? We should have taken it over quietly days ago, and had a curtain placed in front of it.'

'Oh, Mother!' Jackie laughed, feeling better every moment. Now and again, when she thought of Jonathan, there was a twinge of nerves in her stomach. She would just have to avoid going to the Lodge in future, and really get down to some work.

But when they arrived at Merton Lodge, they found that the Brigadier, and Mrs Nelson, had put on a festive occasion, and they were welcomed in with a great deal of gaiety.

The 'unveiling', however, was merely accomplished by Jonathan carrying in the picture from the back of their small car and placing it on a chair for them all to stand back and admire.

'It's splendid, my dear,' said Brigadier Nelson, after a small silence. 'Just what I wanted. You've captured the sunshine, and I always think of the place bathed in sunshine. It will give Evelyn and me a great deal of pleasure.'

'Thank you,' said Jackie, rather huskily, moved by the sincerity in his voice. It was well worth all the special effort she had made.

She was very conscious of Jonathan, looking tall and distinguished in his dark clothes, his black eyes glittering though his face was partly in shadow.

'Jonathan has insisted on champagne,' said Mrs Nelson, laughing.

'We aren't only launching the picture, we must drink to Jackie's success as well,' he said, coming forward. 'At least you're off to a good start.'

It was a mixed evening. Jackie alternately felt elated and full of hope for the future, then a look at Jonathan's brooding face would put a damper on everything. She could not imagine a time when she had not been in love with him. It must have been there all the time, yet it was only when she saw him smiling at Janetta Hodge that she had realised it.

Did the girl mean a lot to him? She had felt there was something between them, but she wondered now, hopefully, if that could not have been her own jealousy.

She was becoming uncomfortably aware, too, of the fact that the Brigadier and Mrs Nelson would not mind fostering a closer relationship between them. Mrs Nelson was not the most subtle of people, and Jackie blushed to hear her own praises being sung to Jonathan, while he scowled a little as she returned the compliment.

'Jackie and I know all about each other, Mother,' he said abruptly. 'I don't suppose anyone knows my faults better.'

'Oh, but you mustn't hide your good qualities either, my dear,' Mrs Nelson put in. 'Must he, Janet?'

She had tried not to influence Jonathan, but it didn't seem to have worked. Now she was following her own inclinations.

'Boys can be a tease sometimes, but they grow out of it . . . '

'I think youngsters are soon aware of their grown-up status,' said Janet, her eyes twinkling. 'Neither Jonathan nor Jackie are exactly children now.'

'No . . . I suppose not.'

'We've been re-designing the walled garden,' said the Brigadier after dinner. 'Perhaps that would give you a few ideas, Jacqueline. I don't know if you enjoy painting gardens and things, but Jonathan could show you anyway.'

Once again the hard look was back on Jon's face, but he rose obediently, and held out a hand to her.

'Why not? Care to come and look,

Jackie? I expect they don't want us to listen to adult conversation in any case.'

There was laughter as Jackie picked up a soft woollen stole. It had been a warm day, but now a cool breeze had sprung up towards evening, and in any case, some of the chill she was feeling came from inside. She was beginning to understand Jon's feelings a little.

She had known the Nelsons for years, and her father and the Brigadier had always been close friends. No doubt they had long since decided that it would be very suitable if their children made a match of it. No doubt, too, Jonathan had been made aware of this long before she had, and was kicking against the idea.

Jackie's cheeks burned as she began to see clearly something to which she had been blind. No wonder Jonathan had been uncomfortable in her company, and when she and her mother had found him in the company of another girl. His own feelings for her were now all too clear, she thought disconsolately.

He must be feeling exasperated and irritated beyond belief at having her thrown at his head!

'That's better,' he said, taking her arm as they went through the small green gate to the walled garden. 'The parents get heavy-handed at times.'

'I know,' she said quietly, 'but don't worry about it, Jon.'

'Worry about it? Look, what do you think of this part of the garden now? Even Father is pleased, and it's been the devil's own job to get him to agree to changes of any kind. I've had to bulldoze him over everything.'

'Then you certainly needn't worry about him bulldozing *you*,' she returned, and he looked at her, puzzled.

But already she was taking in the work which had been done on a very neglected part of the garden, and her natural love for beauty made her exclaim over it.

'Why, Jonathan, it's beautiful! Oh, just look at it from this angle with the evening sun against the trees. It's not really *my* kind of picture, but I wouldn't mind having a go . . . '

She drew back. He would think she was trying to take advantage of a chance to see him again, rather more frequently.

'Though it would have to be in the future. I'm going to do a few sketches and display them in a local shop. They go awfully well when we get visitors.'

'Is that the best way to market your stuff?' he asked. 'It seems to me that you have more talent, or too much talent to allow it all to 'waste its sweetness on the desert air'.'

'I'm not first class, or ever will be,' she said sadly. 'I had to face up to that some time ago, but I think I can paint pictures which please.'

'I think so, too,' he told her gently.

He drew her into his arms, and found her stiff as a ramrod as he tried to kiss her.

'Don't, Jonathan!'

He let her go immediately.

'Is it no use, Jackie?'

51

Tears were threatening, but she felt her misery to be mixed with anger. How dared he think she would just fall into his arms because they all thought it a good idea! Where would it all lead? To a marriage of convenience, while he saw girls like Janetta Hodge when he felt like it?

'There's no need to be a puppet, Jon,' she said quietly. 'We both know it's what the parents want . . . '

'But surely . . . '

'They can throw us at each other's head as much as they like, but we needn't play. For goodness' sake let's be ourselves.'

He was standing beside her quietly and she could see his dark eyes staring into hers.

'Is that how you feel, Jackie? That we're being pushed at one another?'

'You know it's true.'

He turned and she could feel the sudden savage anger in him.

'Yes, damn it! I know it's true. Why couldn't they mind their own business!'

'Then be yourself, as I say. If it's Janetta Hodge you want, then why bother to pay attention to me just to please the parents?'

'Janetta?'

'You looked as though you were . . . special friends. I . . . I thought she was probably in love with you.'

He didn't deny it, but continued to stand with his hands in his pockets, his shoulders hunched.

'And you?'

'Don't you know that for an artist, work must always come first?' she asked lightly.

'So I mean less to you than . . . than the urge to paint this garden?'

She could not answer that.

'There's . . . there's no other man?'

Why should it matter to him if there was?

'No,' she told him briefly.

'Why can't they mind their own business?' he asked, and again she could feel the anger in him.

'Well, I can't see you letting it bother

you. You seem to have managed to impose your own wishes over other things.'

'You disapprove?'

She shrugged. 'It's none of my business.'

'If I didn't, how much do you think would be left when it's my turn to look after the Lodge?' he asked roughly. 'I happen to love the place, and I don't want to inherit a ruin.'

'Of course not,' she agreed quietly.

Yet she could not help remembering the small signs which showed that the Brigadier could not be too lavish with his money. Did Jonathan take that into consideration?

'It's growing colder,' she said, pulling her stole more closely round her shoulders. 'I think I would like to go in now.'

'All right.'

Again he took her arm, then suddenly he pulled her to him and kissed her.

'That's just to say goodnight.'

'Leave me alone,' she said, her heart racing madly. She was glad that it was now so dark that he couldn't see how much she was moved.

'Sorry, Jackie. That was stupid of me.'

The parents looked up expectantly as they both returned, but apart from flags of colour in her cheeks, and a spark of anger in her eyes, Jacqueline had hold of herself again.

'Your garden is lovely now,' she told Brigadier Nelson, 'but it wouldn't really make the sort of painting I like to do.'

'Pity,' he said, disappointed, though his shrewd eyes said that he could have been referring to something else.

'We must go now,' said Janet, rising. She always knew when Jackie was upset. 'You must come over to the cottage one evening soon.'

'Make it afternoon,' said the Brigadier. 'It's a long time since I had a look at the place again, and Jackie's picture has put the notion on me.'

'All right,' laughed Janet. 'You can all come to tea next Thursday.'

'I must make my apologies,' said Jon swiftly. 'You forget, I'm a working man now.'

'But Bruce and I are delighted to come,' said his mother.

'Of course we are. Goodnight, Jackie my dear. You've given me a lot of pleasure.'

He looked suddenly rather old, and the young girl reached up to kiss his cheek, then stared at Jonathan. Things had got into a mess, she thought miserably. Why did she have to go and fall in love with Jonathan?

3

It was difficult to turn her attention to more work, thought Jackie, over the next few days. Her cheque would not last very long and she would have to dip into the savings account her father had helped her to build up over the years for any extra expenses.

Another letter came from Aunt Maude, addressed to her this time, and Jackie opened it while she and her mother were having breakfast.

This time it was rather brief and to the point. Maude and Hetty would be very grateful if Jackie would come and stay, even if only for two weeks, and without Janet if she could not spare the time. If she wanted to work, Maude was sure there was a good market for seascapes as she had seen several on display, painted on the spot, at places like Brixham.

'What do you think, Mother?' asked Jackie, feeling laughter bubbling inside for the first time since she had been to the Lodge. 'Should I exchange landscapes for seascapes and paint harbour scenes instead of Cotswold villages?'

Janet hesitated. She did not really want Jackie to go away so soon after coming home from college, but she would have to be very blind not to notice that something had happened between her daughter and Jonathan Nelson. Perhaps it would do her good to get away for a week or two, especially to a place like Torbay.

'I think it might be a good idea,' she agreed, and passed the letter she had been reading back to Jackie. 'I think you ought to feel flattered that the aunts want you so badly. They've always seemed so self-sufficient.'

'Yes.'

Jackie frowned and read the letter again. Wasn't there rather a lot of urgency in it? Or could it just be that they were missing her company this year, or the company of so many guests? Perhaps they were finding their new house rather lonely.

Jackie gave a thought to the new house, and found her curiosity stirring as she wondered what it was like. They had a wonderful view of the bay at Goodrington, or so she understood from their letters. Surely they would both be contented to enjoy the sunshine in their garden, especially since they would now have more time to attend to it. Hetty had always deplored the fact that the boarding house had not enough garden, but she had placed tubs and urns, overflowing with flowers, at strategic places all over their small concrete yard, and had encouraged climbing roses and clematis to riot over the white walls of the house. Maude had helped as best she could, but always under Hetty's guidance.

'I wonder if their telephone is connected yet,' she mused. 'That's another puzzle. They were so insistent that they would be free of the telephone when they retired, since it used to keep ringing so often, but now they've decided to get it installed again.'

'If you ask me, they're finding retirement not quite the paradise they had expected,' said her mother. 'I don't think they've the natures for it.'

'I don't know,' said Jackie thoughtfully. 'They have plenty of hobbies. Hetty has her garden and she loves cooking, while Maude does marvellous petit point and gros point. They used to love to get their feet up in the evenings. Anyway, which day should I travel? Thursday? I could go by train . . . '

'No, take the Mini,' said Janet. 'I shan't need it.'

'But what if you want to go to Bristol or Bath?'

'I can go with Elsie Bucknill if I want. No, dear, you'll need to take down your paints and things, so take the Mini.'

'Then I'll make it Thursday, and miss the week-end traffic.'

'Don't stay away too long,' said her

mother, as she cleared the table. 'Don't get too good at seascapes and become another Turner!'

'Oh, Mum! Stop pulling my leg!'

Jackie had chosen another hot day to travel to Goodrington, and the small car felt airless, even with the windows open. She made for Bath, and the miles which lay ahead towards the Exeter by-pass.

She had not seen Jonathan again, and had deliberated a little over telephoning to say goodbye. Then she felt a bit silly. It was not as though she was going for ever!

Though, as far as Jonathan was concerned, it might as well be as final. No doubt he would soon be engaged to Janetta, or to some other girl she didn't know about, now that he felt free of any obligation towards her.

Jackie began to welcome the change, feeling that if she got well away from Jonathan, she would be able to see her own life much more clearly and could plan what she wanted to do with herself without her mind always switching to Jonathan and what might have been, if only her heart had been satisfied.

Her other concern had been leaving Janet, but her mother had quickly dispelled any worries on that account.

'How do you think I managed while you were at college?' she asked laughingly.

'Of course — I almost forgot,' said Jackie.

In fact, she wondered a little if Janet would not prefer to have the cottage to herself again, for a little while. Perhaps she had grown away from home while she was at College.

'I shall miss you, though,' said her mother sincerely, and Jackie nodded. They would always be very close.

Jackie drove into Torquay, then along through Paignton to Goodrington. She had always loved coming here to help the aunts, revelling in the beauty of the place. Today it was looking its best, and her spirits lifted even as she began to look for signs which would pinpoint the new house.

Twice she had to ask for guidance, and at last she stopped in front of a small house, with a pretty garden in which she could see Aunt Hetty's energetic fingers had already been employed. It was solidly built, its façade painted the delicate pink which Aunt Maude loved, and pretty fresh frilled curtains at the window.

She saw one twitch, then a moment later the door opened, and both aunts arrived down the path to greet her. Aunt Maude was the small one and more slender than her sister, but she was also the more dominant of the two. But it was Hetty who clasped her warmly and who seemed to be most relieved that she had come.

'I'm sure everything will be all right now,' she said happily.

Jackie did not miss the warning look Maude shot at her sister, and her curiosity was stirred. There *was* something wrong. She had felt it from the tone of their letters, but she also knew that she would have to bide her time before they told her about it. If she came straight out with it, and asked them for an explanation, they would both retreat in horror, and deny the lot! They hated discussing their affairs until they were ready to do so.

'How is Janet?' asked Maude. 'I didn't think she'd want to come with you. Richard always had trouble winkling her out of her own home. She just likes pottering about in her own little groove.'

Jackie laughed. Her mother and the aunts had no illusions about one another.

'She's very well, and the cottage looks lovely, though your new house, here, looks lovely too. Are you happy with it?'

For a moment it looked as though she had taken the breath out of them both, then they hurried to speak at the same time.

'Of course, dear.'

'It's just what we always wanted,' said

Maude, with enthusiasm. 'It's quite small and compact after the boarding house, yet it feels spacious and comfortable, too. And you can see that it's strongly built . . . '

'And such a view!' put in Hetty.

'Yes, it is wonderful,' said Jackie, going over to the sitting-room window to look out at the bay with the lovely view of the sea beyond. She was glad she had brought her working materials. Here, surely, she could do some good work.

Her thoughts returned again to the aunts, who were standing side by side, surveying her anxiously. The sitting-room was delightful, decorated in soft green and grey with one or two pieces of furniture which Aunt Maude treasured, though for the most part it was new to Jackie.

'You must show me round after I've had a wash,' she said, and Hetty leapt into action.

'Oh, my dear, we are slow in giving you a proper welcome! Maude will take you up to your bedroom and show you the bathroom, and I'll have tea ready in a few minutes, then you can see over the house properly.'

'All right, Aunt Het. Oh, and Mother has sent you this basket of things from home . . . jams and preserves, and eggs from the farm nearby. She has made most of the things herself.'

It was a happy tea table, and the aunts began to seem much more like their old selves. Jackie had seen signs of nervousness in them both at first, in their hurried movements and slight forgetfulness, but over tea they were talking quite naturally again, and relaxing down to enjoy it all, much as they had done in the old days.

'I must say it feels good to sit down to a meal, and know we needn't jump up and rush off to attend to something for our guests,' said Hetty, happily cutting herself a slice of Janet's fruit cake.

'Hetty, you'll put on more weight,' said Maude.

'At my age, who cares?' asked her sister. 'I'm not likely to have any man chasing after me!'

There was heavy silence, and Jackie felt her face go hot. Had the aunts heard anything about Jonathan? But there was nothing to tell, and she could not imagine Janet writing to them about him. Janet would never appeal to the aunts to help with any problem, even if there had been one.

Then she saw that it was Aunt Maude whose face wore a closed look, and Jackie pondered, even as she asked for another cup of tea. Could some man have been paying Aunt Maude attention and was Hetty jealous? They were both in their sixties, which was an age when one was as young as one felt, but they were now rather set in their ways. A man's intrusion into such a household would certainly cause a bit of havoc, especially for the sister who was left!

'Tell me more about the house,' she

invited, and saw that the change of subject was a welcome relief. 'Have you had to sell off some of your old furniture and buy new, or what?'

'Not quite, dear,' said Maude eagerly. 'We sold the boarding house just as it stood, except for our good pieces . . . family things, you know . . . which we wanted to keep. Our buyer was most happy to have it that way. Then we bought Maidenbank as it stood. Silly name, don't you think? Not really appropriate.'

Jackie grinned. Perhaps it was more appropriate than they gave credit for.

'It isn't such a bad name for the house,' she said. 'Quite pretty.'

'We'll change it when we can think of another,' said Hetty. 'Of course we made changes in the house. The last people had let it to holiday visitors during the summer months, you see. For years. Some people used to come here year after year, just as they did to us, I suppose. In fact . . . '

She stopped abruptly, looking again

at Maude who was staring at her, stony-faced.

'Have you had people wishing to come back again?' asked Jackie shrewdly.

'Yes,' said Hetty, rather reluctantly, then all in a rush, 'One family. At least, one man who says he's stayed here before with his family. He wanted to come back. Was most insistent. I . . . I didn't like him . . . don't like him.'

'He's a pleasant enough man,' said Maude.

'*Too* pleasant. To you!'

'And you're jealous!'

'Don't be ridiculous!'

Jackie saw that she had now got to the root of the trouble between the aunts. So it *was* a man after all, but a holidaymaker who wanted to return to a house he had known, and no doubt loved. And he had obviously been trying to get round Aunt Maude, and Hetty didn't like it!

'Er . . . have you made many changes?' she asked, leaping in to change the subject, if temporarily. There were obviously strong feelings about it, and the aunts would be finding opportunities to give her their versions, she was very sure.

'Oh, we've only managed to decorate the drawing room, kitchen and bathroom,' said Hetty, 'and we've replaced some of the carpets and curtains. The colours were too strong, though no doubt the last people wanted it all to be hard-wearing and easy to keep clean. People who rent a house don't want to be troubled by housekeeping, do they? And that Mr Naismith was quite rude when he found we *were* decorating the place.'

'He apologised after he had seen what had been done,' put in Maude. 'It was only his bedroom that he liked to see was the same. He was . . . was rather sweet and sentimental about it, I thought. It had happy memories for him since before his wife died, and he didn't want to think of it all being changed.'

'Good heavens, one can't keep a boarding house bedroom always the same because a guest is sentimental about it!'

'This isn't the boarding house now, Hetty.'

'No. It's our home, and all the more reason why we can do what we like with it. I do believe that Naismith man would have imposed on us to give him Jackie's bedroom this week if she had not been coming. Even you found him alarming, Maude.'

'That was just until I got to know him a little better. I . . . I think his nerves have been upset by family troubles, and especially his wife's death. He came down here for his little holiday as usual . . . '

'A long holiday. He's been here nearly a month!'

'Where from?' asked Jackie.

'Liverpool, dear,' said Hetty. 'He has a small printing business there, he tells me, which he runs with his son and daughter. They're coming down soon as well.'

71

'Oh.' Jackie was interested if only because she saw that it had been upsetting in some way for the aunts. 'And where is Mr Naismith staying?' she asked.

'Oh, he's booked in at one of the small hotels nearby, though he passes the house to go down to the bay.'

'He's always hanging around the garden,' said Hetty.

'Only because he's lonely.'

'Well, if we hadn't had years of experience in not being put upon too much, then we'd have had a guest. I'm sure of that,' said Hetty firmly. 'I think he didn't want us to start decorating that bedroom simply because he wanted to stay in it. Give the man an inch and he takes a yard!'

Maude made no reply to that. Obviously, when he found he could not get round both sisters, Mr Naismith had gone all out to charm one of them.

But why? wondered Jackie. Was he really so sentimental that he wanted to come back to this house, even though he knew it had now changed hands?

Jackie rose to help the aunts, deciding to reserve judgement. But if Mr Naismith decided to call again, she would be quite interested to meet him, and to judge whether or not he needed to be shown the door!

Obviously Hetty was wary of him, if not downright scared, though that was probably in case Maude decided he had become a good enough friend to whom to offer hospitality.

And Maude? Could it be that the widower had been paying marked attention to her, and that she could not help being flattered? In the days when she and Hetty were business women with lots of things to attend to, that might not have mattered. But this could be a dangerous time for Maude when she was finding time on her hands.

Jackie looked at both of them. They were her father's only sisters and as unlike Richard Arnold as they were one another. Yet they all had a common factor, a basic sweetness of temperament which made them so lovable, even as she had loved her father.

She was very glad they had asked her to come, she decided.

'Come on,' she said gaily, 'let's look over your new abode. I haven't even glanced at the bedroom you gave me yet.'

It was an interesting house with odd little corners and unexpected angles. Besides the spacious drawing room, there was a small, cosy dining room and a tiny morning room off the kitchen.

'That's for when we want to be alone,' said Maude, with a smile. 'It was one of the attractions for us, wasn't it, Hetty? We always worked well together, but we did like to be on our own from time to time.'

Jackie remembered the small 'office' in the boarding house, and how each of the aunts had gone there to write letters.

'Are you still writing letters?' she asked, and they laughed with one another.

'Even more letters now!' said Hetty.

The kitchen was everything one could wish, in primrose grey and white.

Upstairs there were three solid bedrooms besides the bathroom and Maude and Hetty had each chosen their own without argument. The spare bedroom was the smallest, with a tiny window and sloping walls, but Jackie thought it very charming with the pretty flowered wallpaper and pale blue curtains and bedspread.

'Is that a cupboard?' she asked.

'Er . . . no, dear,' said Maude, 'that's a door, up into the attic. I . . . I did wonder if you would mind. It didn't seem to matter at first, because we thought we were only likely to have you or your mother as guests. But now we wonder if you ought to have Hetty's bedroom or mine.'

'Why ever should I? This is quite big enough, and if there's room in the attic, it can take the overflow of my painting stuff.'

'That's what I thought,' said Hetty,

relieved. 'It's rather dark and gloomy, but it's quite clean. It's been kept well swept, and it's quite empty. The last people didn't believe in keeping things in the attic. They said it was a fire hazard, so if you want to have a look, dear, you'll see it's perfectly all right. I'll go first.'

'No, I'll pop up,' said Jackie, intrigued. 'Save your legs.'

She climbed the solid wooden stairs which were right in front of her when the aunts opened the door. There was faint light from a skylight window, bolted from the inside, and the place was quite empty except for a few packing boxes, but it was well swept as the aunts had said. It would be a splendid store place for extra materials, such as wood to make frames for her canvas to be nailed on, and paint cleaning materials. There was a faint, but not unpleasant odour.

'What's the niff?' she asked, coming back downstairs.

'Oh, we had it all sprayed against

woodworm,' said Hetty. 'I was afraid the beams might be affected a little. You're sure you won't be nervous of the attic, dear? There's a key in the door, if you want to keep it locked.'

'No, of course I'm not nervous,' laughed Jackie. 'What could be up there? Ghosts going bump in the night?'

The aunts gave a flickering glance at one another, then laughed loudly.

'Well, we haven't yet seen a ghost,' said Maude. 'I'll help you with the rest of your things out of the car. There's plenty of hot water, dear, so you can have a bath any time.'

'I shall have it now,' said Jackie, and as they walked into the drawing room, she went over to look again at the beautiful view.

'Thank you for asking me,' she told them both, sincerely. 'I'm going to love it here.'

'We . . . we hope so, don't we, Maude?' said Hetty.

'We do indeed,' said Maude.

Jackie was up early the following morning, encouraged by the warm bright sunshine washing in her bedroom window. She lay for a moment listening to the early morning sounds coming from the kitchen, thinking that old habits die hard. In spite of retirement, the aunts obviously still preferred to get up at the crack of dawn!

Jackie pulled on her jeans and T-shirt, tying back her soft fair hair into a ponytail, then ran lightly downstairs to the kitchen.

'Good morning, Aunt Maude, Aunt Hetty. Isn't it glorious?'

'You'll need a hat, dear,' said Hetty. 'The sun can get very hot.'

Jackie nodded, having been advised on hats for years.

'Can I help?' she offered. 'Is it brasses and silver today?'

It had been one of her chores at the boarding house, and was one of her least favourite tasks, but Hetty was shaking her head.

'We did them all yesterday, and anyway, this time you're on holiday.'

'Then it will have to be a different sort of work,' Jackie decided. 'I mean to capture your view of the bay. Can I sit in that side garden? I've got a canvas already stretched, just about the size I need.'

Maude was interested in Jackie's work, and liked to encourage her.

'I'll help you carry out your things,' she offered, 'and you may have one of these chairs, if you like.'

An hour later Jackie was absorbed in her work, and had lightly pencilled in the outline of her picture, when she was startled by a man's voice hailing Aunt Maude.

'Good morning, Miss Arnold! What a pity you don't have a dog.'

Maude had been industriously polishing the front door knocker, and Hetty was busy in the kitchen behind Jackie. She could hear Hetty exclaim with impatience as Maude walked down the garden path to the gate.

'A dog, Mr Naismith? For protection, you mean?'

'No, Miss Maude. For companionship. Then I could take him a walk for you round the bay. Unless you . . .'

'Oh no, Mr Naismith, I couldn't possibly. Er . . . we have a guest, you see.'

'A guest?'

Jackie heard the sharp note in the man's voice, and put down her tear-off palette board, wiping her fingers on a rag. Then she walked along the side garden to the front of the house, where a tall well-built man with greying hair was talking to her aunt.

'My niece, Jackie. Miss Jacqueline Arnold. Ah, my dear, this is Mr Naismith, who is here on holiday.'

'How do you do, Miss Arnold?' said Derek Naismith, holding out a rather flabby hand. 'Dear me, *three* Miss Arnolds now! I shall have to call you Maude, Hetty and Jackie . . . to distinguish you, of course.'

'I see you're enjoying the morning sunshine and fresh air, Mr Naismith,' said Hetty, rather flatly, behind them. 'It's quite the best time of day and you're wise to take the benefit of it when you've got the time to do so. Unfortunately we ladies aren't free at the moment. Our niece is an artist, a professional artist . . . '

'Oh now, that *does* interest me,' said Derek Naismith with enthusiasm. 'My son is keenly interested in art. He and my daughter are coming down to stay next week, so I hope he'll have the pleasure of meeting you, Miss . . . er . . . Miss Jackie. I've booked rooms for them at my hotel. At one time we used to stay in this house, Miss Jackie, and enjoyed it all so much.'

'I've made the coffee,' said Hetty clearly.

'Ah, I can smell the aroma. Miss Maude . . . '

'Would you care for some coffee, Mr Naismith?' asked Maude politely, and

Hetty glared. Jackie hid a smile, though she was beginning to see why Hetty could not stand Mr Naismith, and wanted some support. She found him much too oily for her own liking. Yet he was paying marked attention to Maude, telling her how the sunshine had brought a becoming tan to her delicate skin.

'My wife was so like you, Maude . . . Miss Maude,' he was saying. 'She used to have trouble with her skin when the sun was too hot. She had the same delicacy as you, though your sort of complexion always looks like apple blossom.'

'I don't think complexion problems trouble us at *our* age,' put in Hetty, 'though I've told Jackie to be careful to wear a hat.'

★   ★   ★

Derek Naismith rose to leave almost reluctantly after drinking his coffee, though he could not fail to realise that he was not altogether welcome as far as Hetty was concerned. His whole attention, however, seemed to be centred on Maude, who turned rather apologetically to Jackie after he had gone.

'I can't help feeling sorry for him, my dear. He and his wife must have been very close and . . . well, it seems that I bear some sort of resemblance to her.'

'She was probably old enough to be your daughter,' said Hetty.

'I don't think age has anything to do with it,' Maude sounded rather offended.

'Well, it has. One must keep a sense of proportion in our position. If you ask me, that Naismith is a rogue and has some scheme up his sleeve. He's after some easy money.'

'Well, I don't know how you can imagine that he imagines he'll find it here.'

Hetty took a moment to think about that.

'Neither do I. But he does, nevertheless. He's a rogue, Maude, and you shouldn't let him in the house.'

'It would probably have been very different if his wife had been like *you*.'

Jackie could see another quarrel brewing up, and she hastily sought around for a change of subject.

'Er . . . is it all right if I work inside later on? When the breeze gets strong it's rather difficult outside. I'll spread down plenty of papers.'

'Of course, Jackie dear,' said Maude. 'We'll be most interested to see what you're doing.'

'Well, I'll just go and put in a bit more work, if I may,' Jackie excused herself, rising. No doubt the aunts would go back to their respective tasks.

Nevertheless, as she took up her paintbrush again, there was a feeling of unease in her heart. Which of the aunts was right? she wondered. Was Derek Naismith just a lonely man, trying to get over the death of his wife, or was he a rogue trying to worm his way into the household for his own purpose? Did he imagine that the aunts had a nice nest egg tucked away now that they had retired, and sold their boarding house very profitably? Surely he could see that they were not gullible women who could be easily cheated, especially when she had also come to stay. It was usually elderly gentle ladies on their own who fell prey to confidence tricksters.

Yet he had seemed to welcome her presence in the house, and was keen for her to meet his son and daughter when they came on holiday.

'Adrian is interested in colour printing,' he had told her. 'He'll be most interested in your art, and will probably be coaxing you to paint him a picture from which he can make some prints. You'll have to go into business together and make a fortune.'

She had treated that as a joke, but she found her interest stirred by the printing business Mr Naismith had mentioned. Perhaps it was her own interest in line, colour and design which attracted her to printing as well as art, and some of her greatest pleasure came from the feel of a brand new book in her hands, and she would often sniff the lingering odour of printer's ink. Maybe this young man would be an interesting companion, and would take her mind off Jonathan. Sitting in the cottage garden, and looking down at the lovely bay, he seemed many miles away.

That evening, however, it was as though he was beside her, when Aunt Maude came to tell her she was wanted on the telephone.

'Why didn't you tell me you were leaving?' asked Jonathan.

'I . . . I didn't know if it would interest you.'

'Not interest me!'

'How is your friend, Miss Hodge?' she cut in, quickly, and there was silence for a moment.

'Very well.'

'I'm glad.'

'Jackie! I rather wanted to talk to you again.'

'Well, say on.'

'Not here. Not on the telephone.'

'I shan't be home for a week or two.' She lowered her voice a little. 'I rather think the aunts need me.'

Again she could hear his soft breathing.

'Is there something troubling you? Or them?'

'N . . . no, not really. Nothing which won't be put right soon, I'm sure. Just a guest who wishes he was still a guest.'

'That sounds very odd.'

She laughed a little.

'It isn't really, but I'll be staying on just the same, Jonathan.'

'I'll look in on your mother now and again,' he offered, and she thanked him as she replaced the receiver. Again he seemed very far away, and as she walked through to the sitting-room, the small house suddenly seemed strange and unreal. She would have to get used to the fact that it now belonged to the aunts, and that the familiar old boarding house was no longer their home.

'The sun has made me sleepy,' she excused herself to them. 'I think I'll go up, if I may.'

'I'll bring you up some hot milk,' offered Aunt Hetty. 'Have a good sleep, dear.'

Maude wished her goodnight, too, though rather absently. She had been very quiet all evening.

In her small pretty bedroom, Jackie quickly drew her curtains, feeling suddenly nervous, as though there were many eyes peering into her lighted bedroom. Or even just one pair!

She felt silly and stupid for feeling so nervous. Why, she had never been nervous in a house in all her life, and this was far from being some sort of ancient property with low ceilings, creaking boards and shadowy corners. This was a very ordinary, bright and pleasant house.

She went over to the attic door and opened it, the faint odour of mustiness mixed with woodworm killer wafting into the room. Quickly she locked it again, and put the key under her pillow, feeling foolish again. How could anyone come into her bedroom out of the attic!

Yet, tired as she was, it was some time before she fell asleep to dream that she was being pursued by Derek Naismith and a small dog, and Jonathan refused to wait for her, and give her a helping hand. When she woke, there were tears on her cheeks, but soon she saw that the sunshine was again lighting up the window and that a new day had dawned.

Feeling very foolish indeed, Jackie fumbled under her pillow for the key to the attic door, then hopped out of bed to put it back in the lock, and pull back the curtains.

The soft surge of the sea was reassuring, as was the peace and tranquillity of the scene from her bedroom window.

Jackie's spirits rose again, as she dressed to go downstairs for breakfast.

4

It was a quiet, peaceful weekend. Derek Naismith must have decided to find some other pursuit than walking aimlessly past the house, and on down to the sands. They saw nothing of him, to Hetty's obvious relief, though Jackie noticed that Aunt Maude often gazed searchingly out of the sitting-room window. After a time, however, she too settled down into routine again, and on Saturday evening Jackie decided to go along to Torquay, and left the aunts happily playing their favourite game of Scrabble.

'I shan't be late,' she promised.

'We ought to know more young people to keep you company,' Maude said, rather worriedly. 'Hetty, I don't think 'dunc' is a word.'

'Don't worry. I like being on my own sometimes. It allows me to think, and perhaps to see a little, too. I need some new scenes to stimulate my work.'

'Then you must go to Brixham,' Maude insisted. 'All those lovely boats, and rich colours. I love harbour scenes.'

'All right, darling, but tonight I go into Torquay. I think I shall go for a ride on top of one of the open-air buses.'

But already Aunt Hetty was finding 'ish' to put on the end of 'burn', and with a smile, Jackie slipped out of the door.

It was odd that for the first time, as she mingled with the crowds in Paignton, she felt rather lonely even as she breathed the fresh sea air. When she had been working in the boarding house, there had always been other students to go around with in the evenings, and she had never lacked company at college. Quite often she had enjoyed her own thoughts, but in those days she had belonged entirely to herself. Now, in spite of all she thought and did, she could not keep Jonathan out of her mind for very long. He was taking away her independence, she thought crossly. He was making her dissatisfied with her own company.

It was still early when she returned back home, though this time she found peace and harmony at Maidenbank and her small bedroom was becoming as familiar as her own back home. The attic door was just a door and she did not even give it a thought as she climbed into bed.

This time Jackie slept very soundly, having decided that Jonathan seemed very far away.

The following Tuesday, the aunts and Jackie ate a late lunch after a shopping spree in Torquay. Jackie was working hard on her pictures, but she had run out of some basic materials, and Maude had decided that she needed a new white hat. Her old one was not immaculate, and she considered that a white hat should not be worn, unless it was perfect.

'You need one, too, Hetty,' she prodded.

'I never wear a white hat. I prefer a black one.'

'And wear it for years! Doesn't it occur to you that if it *had* been white, it would have been black by now?'

'It's perfectly clean. I know how to take care of my hats.'

'It's a good job. They have to last you a very long time.'

Jackie allowed the argument to wash over her head. The aunts often bickered amiably and she was glad to hear them at it again. The words which had passed between them over Derek Naismith had been rather different. They had not seen him now for a few days, and Jackie continued to feel relieved. She hoped he had decided to go home to Liverpool, and that the aunts would soon forget all about him.

They all enjoyed their shopping spree and Jackie helped with the choosing of a hat for Aunt Maude. She had a neat head of grey hair, and looked well in a hat. She must have been very attractive when she was young, thought Jackie, and wondered why she had never married. She must ask her mother some time.

She was helping Aunt Hetty to clear up after lunch, when the doorbell shrilled twice.

'Oh dear, I'll go,' said Maude, who had been carefully cleaning her shoes before putting them away. A moment later they could hear Derek Naismith's booming voice and the murmur of other voices.

'Oh, lor!' said Hetty. 'Not that awful man again! I thought we'd got rid of him when you came, Jackie. If Maude encourages him any more, I . . . I shall hit her!'

'I'm afraid he's brought his family with him,' said Jackie, as she heard them all going into the sitting-room.

'I don't know whether that's good or bad,' complained Hetty. 'Good in that he won't be mooning round Maude any more saying how lonely he is since he'll have his son and daughter to entertain him, or bad in that we're likely to be inflicted with all three!'

Jackie laughed outright.

'Oh, Aunt Hetty! You're getting an obsession over Mr Naismith. Surely you've seen worse than he is at the boarding house. He's just an ordinary sort of man.'

'That was work, and they didn't all go smarming over Maude.'

'Surely you *can't* be jealous?'

Hetty looked at her squarely.

'Is that it, do you think, Jackie?' she asked. 'Is my judgement at fault because I'm jealous? Don't you feel there's something not quite right about him?'

Jackie considered thoughtfully.

'People do odd things when they're emotionally upset,' she said. 'I can't judge. Anyway, here's Aunt Maude wanting coffee. We'd best go meet the family.'

Adrian Naismith was about the best-looking young man Jackie had ever seen. Tall, dark, with a faint touch of olive in his skin, it seemed to her that his mother had perhaps been a Latin. But no . . . wasn't she supposed to have been like Aunt Maude? Grandparents, then, she decided, her keen artist's eye on him, seeing the lithe grace as he rose to greet her. There was almost perfection in the modelling of his face, and Jackie suddenly realised that she had been staring at him rather too long. She coloured guiltily, even as she turned to his sister.

She had caught a quick look of satisfaction on Derek Naismith's face, however, and felt chagrined with herself. It was almost as though he were telling her that he knew all along his son would bowl her over.

Cynthia Naismith was quite different from either her father or brother. She was small and plain at first glance, with straight lightish brown hair, a small slender figure and nothing very distinguishable in her features. But Jackie, still feeling uncomfortable at showing her interest in Adrian, shook her by the hand and gave her a specially warm smile.

'How do you do,' she said. 'It's so nice to see another girl here.'

Cynthia stared back at her and for a moment her eyes seemed to come alive, blazing with green light. Jackie caught her breath, for here was no insipid girl. Something in Jackie had aroused strong feelings in her, but whether the girl was glad to meet her or not, she could not decide because in a second, almost, the sulky look was back on her face again.

'How do you do,' she mumbled.

'Yes, I'm sure you will both be splendid company for Jackie,' Aunt Maude was saying, as she poured the coffee.

'Adrian wants to see Jackie's pictures,' said Derek. 'I'm fond of pictures myself and I've got quite a few I've picked up. They're good investment, you know. I've got a nice Canaletto and a Breughel . . . '

Jackie mentally registered that information and decided that Aunt Hetty was off the mark when she suspected

Mr Naismith of fortune-hunting! If he had a few such good pictures, then he could not be hard up!

'Oh yes. You're interested in printing, I believe?' she asked, turning to the young man.

His large black eyes looked into hers.

'Very. I love colour and design. We'll have much in common, Miss . . . is it Arnold?'

'Yes. My aunts are my father's sisters.'

'It's nice to have a family. We three are all that's left of ours.'

'And are you interested in printing, Miss Naismith?'

Cynthia shrugged.

'*Some* printing, yes. I find it very interesting. But I help to run the business side.'

Jackie nodded. She could see shrewdness in the girl and it wouldn't be hard to imagine her keeping control over all the accounts.

'That's the really important part,' she agreed. 'I rather think I need to be more of a business woman to market my work, or I could do with an agent or something.'

'We'll talk about that some time,' said Adrian. 'I'm a business man, too, even if it's the practical side of printing which attracts me.'

'He's learned all there is to learn about it,' said his father proudly.

'You promised we'd go for a swim, Adrian,' said Cynthia, rising.

Her father frowned and Jackie caught a glance which passed between them, almost of dislike. But surely Derek Naismith could not dislike his only daughter! Yet that sort of thing was not unheard-of in families. He obviously adored his son, and perhaps he had given all his love to the boy of the family. Jackie hoped Mrs Naismith had made up for it by loving Cynthia.

She looked at the girl, seeing the carefully deadpan look back on her face. One would expect that if Mr Naismith had missed his wife so much, then he would turn to his daughter for comfort. Yet he had, instead, hung round this house where they had been happy, and gazed on Aunt Maude who bore a resemblance to the dead woman.

Had Cynthia been starved of love over the years? wondered Jackie, puzzled by the girl, and feeling sudden sympathy for her.

'Maybe you could take Jackie,' Derek Naismith was suggesting.

'Oh no, not at the moment,' she said quickly. 'I've still got work to do. Er . . . some other time.'

She felt she had had enough of this family for the moment, as they rose to go.

She felt very conscious of Adrian Naismith as he stood towering over her and as he clasped her hand before leaving.

'I'll call and see you again,' he said, in a low voice.

The house seemed very empty after they had gone and Maude turned almost defiantly to Hetty.

'They seem a very nice family,' she

said. 'I'm glad poor Mr Naismith has someone of his own, especially a daughter to look after him.'

'Hm,' said Hetty, and went to the window to watch them out of sight, Cynthia a tiny slender figure between the other two.

'That girl,' she said. 'Something is wrong about that girl.'

'What?' asked Jackie, interested.

'She's been engaged, for one thing. I saw her rubbing at her finger, and there was a mark where she'd been wearing a ring. I wonder if he gave her the push, or if she threw him over. And I wonder what broke it up. She's only a little thing, but I bet she's the bossy one.'

'Oh, Het! Honestly!' said Maude, but it sounded almost like relief. If Hetty started to pick on Cynthia, then she might leave Derek alone. And in spite of herself, Maude could not help being stirred by the way his eyes lingered on her, even if he was remembering his wife all the time. She must have been a remarkable woman to have commanded such love.

Jackie was hurrying to get on with her work, but she, too, was thinking about the Naismiths. Adrian had a marvellous head. Portraits had never been her strong point, but she had to admit that she would love to try one of him. She would do a portrait of Adrian.

She worked on with enthusiasm, and she was a great deal less lonely. The Naismiths were only different, and she would soon get used to them.

★   ★   ★

Adrian Naismith lost no time in seeking out Jackie the following morning. She had pointed out the side garden from where she was working on her painting, and instead of calling formally at the front door, his head appeared over the solid wall of the garden.

'Hello! Thought I'd find you here.'

'Mr Naismith . . .'

'Adrian. Otherwise we'll just get confused.'

'Adrian, then. What are you doing here?'

He heaved himself up, then leapt over the wall and she saw that he was clad rather less formally, also, in jeans, sweater and leather sandals.

'Coming to look at your picture,' he told her with a grin which showed perfect white teeth.

There was silence while he studied it, and she could not help being aware of his attraction as he stood beside her. Jonathan would be every inch as tall, but his looks were only pleasant beside Adrian Naismith.

'Uh-huh!' he said, and stood back to look down on the bay. 'You've got the gift all right, but you need to do a little more work on it here, and here.'

She was slightly taken aback, having heard no constructive criticism since she left college.

'Think so?' she asked, her attention caught.

'Look for yourself.'

'I thought it wasn't *quite* right, but sometimes one has to wait till the picture is finished.'

'Well, I should lift that a little.'

For a short time they argued, then reached a compromise, and Jackie felt unusually elated. It was seldom she could find anyone to share her absorbing interest in what she was doing, and share it intelligently. Adrian was even going a step further. He was putting her right!

He smiled at her again, his dark eyes raking over her so that she felt suddenly small and rather vulnerable, and for a quick moment, repelled. Then the moment passed, and he was just a nice young man whose company was very welcome.

'You haven't brought your sister, then?'

'Cynthia? No, Dad has latched on to her today, but she'll probably be stinging him for a store load of goods. He can be quite careful with his money until Cynthia goes to work on him.'

Adrian laughed, shaking his head indulgently, and Jackie suddenly felt lonely again. More than once she had thought she would have liked a brother. How nice it would have been, especially now that her father was dead.

'I thought we could go down to the sands for a walk, and a talk, if you like. You intrigue me . . .'

'In what way?'

'A girl of your talents. Most girls can look pretty, and can cook and wash up and go out dancing looking like a million. But not many can put that gorgeous scene on to a bit of canvas, and capture all the life and colour that goes with it, and still look the way you do.'

She could not fail to feel flattered. Jonathan had tried to express his feelings about the picture, but in much less coherent terms. Now, in simple words, Adrian had managed to make her feel a talented and lovely girl.

'I'll just tell the aunts,' she said, her

cheeks happily flushed, 'and change out of these old jeans.'

Something flashed in the dark eyes as he looked after her tall figure, her silky hair bobbing as she ran. A short time later she returned, wearing brief blue shorts and matching sandals, a white sweater round her neck. Her long legs were a pale honey-gold colour, and Adrian did not trouble to hide his admiration.

'Talk about a golden girl!' he said, taking her arm. 'I sure hit gold the day I set eyes on you.'

'You sound as if you mean it,' she said, slightly taken aback again at the fervent note in his voice.

'I do,' said Adrian. 'I do mean it.'

★ ★ ★

It had been just what she needed, thought Jackie later. The fun of walking along the sands with Adrian made her feel more alive than she had done for weeks. There were crowds of people and the air of holiday enjoyment was infectious.

'Where should we go?' asked Adrian, buying her a huge ice cream. 'I got a brochure and it invited me to see flamingoes in the Zoo, visit a model village or ancient caves. Or we can go to Brixham and have a day out fishing for mackerel.'

'It all sounds very exciting, but I said I'd be home for lunch.'

'This afternoon, then!'

Jackie didn't know why she hesitated, and this hesitation reminded her of a similar one with Jonathan. And that time she had regretted it later.

But she felt that Adrian Naismith would sweep her along with him if she didn't watch out, and she was a girl who must always be sure of each step in her life.

'No,' she laughed. 'Not this afternoon either. I really must get my work done.'

For a moment there was a flicker of anger in his dark eyes, as though he wasn't used to being thwarted.

'Surely you can leave it for one day.'

'Oh, if I do that, it's fatal. I'd keep putting off all the time. Besides . . . ' she hesitated, 'I thought you understood.'

Quickly the good-humoured smile was back on his face.

'Of course. And there will be other days. Though *please* try to save a little of each day for me. Remember, I shan't be here very long. Can we go to Brixham tomorrow? Tell the aunts we're out eating a cream tea. I've got a fancy for cream.'

She could see the small boy in him and laughed gaily.

'All right. I'll be free tomorrow afternoon.'

'Be ready at two o'clock.'

'Sharp?'

'Sharp!'

He was nice, she thought, as she swung in the garden gate and waved him away, then she turned to see Aunt Hetty viewing her with concern.

'The father chases after Maude, and

now the son has got his hooks into you,' she said sourly. 'I'll be having the girl offering to wind my wool for me next.'

'Oh, Aunt Hetty!' cried Jackie crossly, 'if you don't let up, you'll be ill. There's nothing wrong with the Naismiths that a little bit of . . . of friendship won't cure!'

She walked indoors as Hetty made no reply, then she glanced back for a moment, catching a rather stricken look on her aunt's face, and the bowed shoulders which made her seem suddenly old. She wanted to go back and say she was sorry, but after a slight hesitation, she walked on. Hetty *did* have an obsession about the Naismiths. It was time she got over it.

* * *

The weather seemed to reflect her mood, thought Jackie, a few days later. Adrian Naismith had called on her the following day and had left her in no doubt that he wanted nothing so much as her company.

'You go, my dear,' Aunt Maude insisted. 'After all, this is meant to be a holiday for you, a sort of thank-you for past years when you helped us so much.'

'You paid me, Aunt Maude.'

'Yes, but you did so much more than anyone else we might have engaged. It was different having you. And I'm sure young Mr Naismith is very nice. It's sort of . . . well, different when we know the whole family.'

Jackie grinned. Aunt Maude didn't approve of pick-ups. You never knew who they were!

But when Adrian called, looking smart in his casual trousers and good sports coat, Maude could only beam with approval.

'Father and Cynthia are hoping to call later,' he told the aunts. 'Father would like to take you both out for tea.'

Even Hetty could find no fault with this, but after the young people had gone she decided that she must finish her strawberry preserves. It was all right for Maude to go, though, especially since Cynthia would be there, too.

'Oh, but Miss Hetty!' protested Derek, 'of course you must come. This was to be a treat for both of you.'

'It will be all the bigger treat for Maude,' said Hetty, 'and do me a favour, too. I like the house to myself when I make my preserves. They have to last all winter and a failure means disappointment later.'

She saw Cynthia looking at her, a Mona Lisa sort of smile on her face. Why did this family irritate her so much? Yet she had to confess that she could find no fault with young Adrian when he had taken Jackie away earlier in the day. He had been charming to her, but she felt that the girl could be a sharp-tongued lass given the opportunity. She might even be impertinent to her father, if she wished. Hetty felt she knew the type, and that the girl was discontented and spoilt.

'Don't you *ever* go out, Miss

Arnold?' she was asking.

'Certainly. But nowhere to meet with *your* approval, I'm sure. I go marketing for the food and I go to church on Sundays.'

Cynthia made a face and Maude leapt in before there were further exchanges.

'I'll get ready, Mr Naismith. This is really very kind of you, to find time for someone like me when you're on holiday.'

'A holiday should be a time for doing as you please,' said Derek grandly, 'and it pleases me to take you out.'

'I wonder where Adrian has gone. And Jackie,' said Cynthia, turning to look rather slyly at her father.

He flushed angrily.

'You keep out of Adrian's affairs,' he told her. 'They'll be enjoying the sunshine and fresh air. Like you should be doing.'

'I wasn't asked,' she said, 'was I?'

Derek turned with relief when Maude came into the room, dressed in her good navy suit and pale blue hat trimmed with forget-me-nots. Hetty could see the girl raise her eyes to the ceiling as she trailed after them, and had sudden sympathy for her. Perhaps her engagement had only just been broken and she was having to get over it in her own way.

She was the odd one out in the family, now that her brother was spending his time with Jackie.

★   ★   ★

Life was good, thought Jackie, as she and Adrian strolled along the side of the harbour at Brixham. The sun beat down on her bare arms and legs and shimmered on her hair like beams of silver. Adrian had taken her hand, his dark good looks complementing her own fair colouring, so that they drew attention as they mingled with the crowds.

Jackie's passion for line and colour was satisfied as she gazed down at all the tiny boats bobbing about in the harbour.

'It looks marvellous,' she said. 'If only I could capture it! But I couldn't . . . the life would be out of it. It takes this sort of scene to show me my limitations . . . good for me, I expect.'

'That's the sort of talk I won't listen to,' said Adrian. 'We'll come back next week, and this time we will load up the car with your canvas, paints and things, then you can see just how good you are. Maybe you'll surprise yourself.'

She laughed happily. Maybe she would. On a day like this anything seemed possible.

'Oh, look!' she cried, as the sea boiled with shoals of tiny fish. 'How could I capture that?'

'It would be there, the life and laughter, if you felt happy inside when you painted it.' He gazed at her intently. 'You *are* happy, aren't you, Jackie?'

'Yes. Why?'

'Oh, I dunno. Somehow you didn't seem to be awfully happy when I first saw you. There was a kind of brooding look on your face, as though you had things on your mind. Did you?'

She thought about Jonathan.

'Perhaps.'

'A man?'

'Perhaps.'

'Have I helped to chase him away? I'd feel happy, too, if I thought I could do that, Jackie.'

'I don't think it's the sort of day to be miserable,' she said, lifting her face to the sun. 'I'm just enjoying being here.'

'But in the right company,' he persisted.

'In good company,' she agreed. 'Let's walk on up that hill, then we can get a marvellous view of Torbay.'

He looked a trifle sulky.

'Oh, Adrian, we hardly know one another. A week ago I didn't know you existed.'

'One can get to know a person in five minutes. You like that person, or you don't. I could tell immediately about you.'

'Well, I'm not like that,' she assured him. 'I'm far more cautious. Sorry, Adrian, but I won't be rushed. I like being out with you, though. Can't we be good companions?'

He was smiling again.

'Of course. Sorry. You shouldn't be so lovely, that's all.'

She felt herself colouring. Was she lovely to Adrian? He was certainly very good-looking, she thought, glancing at his profile. He must have had lots of girls attracted to him.

'What about that tea, with lots of Cornish cream?' he asked, 'or is it Devon cream?'

'You'll fatten us both up,' she laughed, 'but I'm on. Let's just admire this view, then we can find somewhere. Oh, goodness, I wonder if I could paint it from this spot. Right here. Isn't it marvellous?'

'Marvellous.'

'I wouldn't mind having a go at you, too, Adrian,' she said, rather shyly, 'though I'm not very good on portraits.

But I would find you interesting to do.'

This time he looked delighted.

'Now that's something I like to hear. I can come every day and sit for you. As a matter of fact, I wouldn't mind giving you the job as a commission, if I can keep the picture. How about it, Jackie? Is it a deal?'

'We'll see how it turns out,' she promised. 'If you like it, then we can come to some arrangement.'

'Excellent. I think I shall have to arrange with Father and Cynthia to stay on an extra week. This is too much fun to leave.'

The days were galloping past, thought Jackie. It would be nice if Adrian could stay longer.

'Tell me about your job in Liverpool,' she said, when they had found a restaurant and ordered tea. 'Is yours a big firm?'

'Heavens, no, it's a fairly small printing plant, but we're kept pretty busy.'

'You and your father run it, and

Cynthia is in charge of the office?'

'That's it, though we have . . . others . . . working for us, too.'

'Did your mother help before Cynthia?'

'Mother?' Adrian looked blank. 'What about Mother?'

'Your father said she died recently.'

'That's it. Just before he came down here.'

'You and your sister must miss her a lot, too.'

'Oh, sure. Sure we do,' said Adrian.

'And your father. Was she really like Aunt Maude? Younger, of course.'

Adrian was looking uncomfortable.

'Er . . . I'd rather not talk about her if you don't mind, Jackie.'

She coloured. 'Oh, sorry. I . . . I didn't know you minded.'

'If you're ready, maybe we'd better go back. Cynthia wants to go ten-pin bowling tonight. I said I'd take her.'

'Of course.'

As they neared home, however, Adrian stopped the car, and in an

118

almost businesslike way, he reached for Jackie and kissed her.

She pushed him away, with the sudden feeling that he must have done this many times before with other girls.

'Don't do that, Adrian. I hate being kissed casually.'

'Then let's make it less casual.'

He reached for her again, and flags of colour rose in her cheeks.

'I meant it.'

He looked sulky again, and turned to start up the car, driving her home in silence.

'See you tomorrow,' he said, as she got out at Maidenbank.

'If you like.'

He reached out and caught her hand, his teeth white as he smiled at her.

'Sorry, my dear, we'll just have to get used to one another. But I intend us to be friends just the same. See you tomorrow, as I say.'

She nodded, and made for the house. It had been a day full of joy, with a sprinkling or two of irritation thrown in. Why was it that nothing ever seemed perfect? Maybe because she expected too much, thought Jackie.

And she did not always understand people, nor did they understand her. Especially her men friends!

5

Janet wrote at least once a week. She hated long conversations on the telephone, and preferred to put all her news on paper. Jackie would have liked to hear about Jonathan, but it was not until the following Monday, when she received her usual letter, that there was news of him.

'Evelyn and Bruce called yesterday,' she wrote, 'and they seem to be rather concerned about Jonathan . . . or rather, that girl he's taking about . . . you know, the one we met. I think her name is Janetta Hodge. Evelyn thinks Jonathan is being too indulgent over her, and that she's an extravagant girl. I hope Jonathan will soon sow his wild oats and start being more considerate towards his parents. He calls in to see me from time to time, though, and I must say he does his best to be charming and considerate . . . '

So why criticise him? thought Jackie. Then she felt her heart sinking a little, that Jonathan had, in fact, turned to Janetta Hodge. She had been right in thinking that it was really that girl who held his heart.

Jackie pulled herself together. Nothing had changed, but she felt rather dismayed as she realised just how much Jonathan still meant to her.

Deliberately she thought again about Adrian, who was coming to sit for her that afternoon. Maude was most interested in the possibility of the portrait, but Hetty had gone rather quiet again. The Naismiths were becoming regular visitors to the house, and although Aunt Hetty was not now viewing Derek with active dislike, Jackie had a feeling that she was only tolerating all three.

Cynthia was one of the most silent girls Jackie had ever met, and on the rare occasions when they were alone, she could not get the girl to talk about herself at all.

'You must come along with Adrian when he sits for me,' she invited. 'It can't be much fun for you with only your father for company when you go down to the sea front. Though, of course,' she added, hastily, 'your father must be very glad of your company now that he's on his own.'

'Oh, very glad,' said Cynthia heavily.

'It's a pity one of your boy-friends wasn't having a holiday down here at the same time. Is there anyone special, Cynthia?'

'Very special,' said Cynthia promptly. 'Unfortunately he's got his claws into someone else at the moment, but he'll soon come crawling back. He always does.'

Jackie thought of the tell-tale mark on Cynthia's finger which Aunt Hetty's sharp eyes had spotted. She began to see a reason for Cynthia's broken engagement.

'Would you want to marry someone

who might go off with another woman?' she asked.

Cynthia shrugged.

'That would depend on how well I knew him,' she said, and there was an odd gleam of concealed amusement on her face. Jackie found herself colouring. It was as though Cynthia was well aware that she was fishing, and was going to give nothing away!

'I could never get to know her,' thought Jackie.

Nor could she ever take a liking to the girl and in this she joined Aunt Hetty. There was something about Cynthia's impassiveness and the secrets which always seemed to be in her eyes which repelled them both. Jackie had been prepared to be sorry for her, but she could see her sympathy was wasted.

When Adrian turned up for his first sitting, he was alone. The weather had changed, and the warm blue skies were dulled with clouds.

'We'll have to work indoors,' said

Jackie. 'What a pity! I would have liked to paint you wearing that yellow open-necked shirt, against the clear blue of the sky. It would have captured the essence of summer.'

'And instead I'm wearing a very ordinary dark suit and an equally ordinary cream shirt. How disappointing for you, darling.'

She blushed. She knew that it was her artist's eye which admired his looks, seeing him in various settings, but now she wondered if Adrian thought it was the woman in her which was seeing him like that. Perhaps she had given that impression once before when he had tried to kiss her.

Now she grew very businesslike, deliberately looking him over.

'As a matter of fact, I think I like that better. A formal portrait could easily be best. Look this way, Adrian, until I see which angle would be most effective . . .'

'Don't you have a studio upstairs?' he asked.

'Goodness, no! This isn't the boarding house. It's only small.'

'I know. I've stayed in it before. Surely you could combine your bedroom with a studio for when the weather is bad?'

'Not enough light. It's only a small window. No, the aunts allow me to use this room. I spread down plenty of newspapers.'

She had been working for almost an hour when the aunts came back from a shopping expedition, and work had to be suspended. Adrian looked a trifle disgruntled again, and Jackie had been hopeful that he might suggest an evening out for them both. But he merely looked rather sulky when she saw him to the door.

'Did I make you sit too long?' she asked. 'I'm sorry. It isn't easy to be a model. I know, because sometimes we modelled for each other at college.'

'How much progress will you make with the two old aunties butting in all the time?' he asked. 'I expect they'll be

126

sitting in their chairs, with their knitting, just behind you next time, watching every brush stroke. You should have a bit of sense and get yourself a proper studio.'

'It isn't my house,' she said quietly. 'I'm only here for a few weeks anyway, and come to that, you'll be away by another week, won't you? Goodness, I'll have to work hard on this. There isn't much time. Can you come again tomorrow, Adrian?'

How moody he was, she thought, seeing his good-looking face rather marred by a scowl.

'I can't talk to you if they're around. It's a wasted day.'

'I thought you wanted a portrait.'

'I want to get to know you better. I want us to have time for one another . . . on our own. Is that unusual, Jackie?'

She didn't know what to say. Did she want to be alone too much with Adrian Naismith? She admired his good looks and had enjoyed his company, but as she had told him once before, she hated to be rushed.

Yet he would soon be going away again, back to his printing job in Liverpool.

'You can arrange it better, Jackie,' he urged her with a grin. 'Just our luck, getting poorer weather. Where is there to go when it rains?'

'It's only raining in showers.'

'I'll come back tomorrow, only get rid of the two old dears. I'll sit for you, but I want to get to know you, Jackie, to find out more about you. And we can't . . . well, talk with their ears flapping all the time.'

She laughed. She could hardly deny that Aunt Hetty's ears flapped. Adrian had the brooding look back on his face.

'Be seeing you,' he said, and slouched away.

'That young man has no manners,' said Aunt Hetty. 'I don't think he said good afternoon to us, or thank us for having him.'

'Oh, Auntie! I think he was just tired,'

Jackie defended. 'I kept him sitting rather a long time.'

'I don't trust him,' said Hetty. 'I don't trust any of them . . . '

'We *know*, dear,' said Jackie. Would Hetty never give up?

That evening, as Jackie prepared to go to bed, she found that her mind was unsettled. She kept thinking about Jonathan, and imagining him smiling across the small table in the restaurant at Janetta Hodge, who was looking very beautiful and self-assured. In Jackie's imaginings she had developed even more poise and elegance.

She slipped down under the covers and tried to shut out these memories, and see Adrian Naismith in his more happy moments when they walked in the sunshine and enjoyed each other's company.

Then Cynthia's face, with its small sly smile, intruded, and she shivered. Was she deliberately holding Adrian at arm's length because she didn't like his family? Did he sense something of the kind and resent it, and even try to turn the tables a little by complaining about the aunts? She should appreciate Adrian for himself, Jackie reminded herself. If she enjoyed his company, then she should forget about his sister and father.

She willed herself to sleep, then she was startlingly awake, hearing faint bumping sounds from the ceiling above. The rain had cleared and the wind died down, so it wasn't anything being blown about, thought Jackie, her skin crawling a little.

She listened intently until her own heartbeats sounded like the big drum in a pipe band, and again she could hear the faint dull thuds from somewhere above the attic stairs.

Jackie leapt out of bed and locked the attic door, then she fumbled in her small jewellery box for a fine silver chain, and hung the key round her neck before crawling back into bed. Whatever Thing was up there, it could not get into her room. She lay trembling with cold and fright, wondering if she ought to run into the next bedroom and wake Aunt Maude. But if she was already asleep, it would be unfair to frighten her. Obviously they hadn't heard, or there would have been movements from their rooms.

The sounds had not been repeated and after a while Jackie began to think she had imagined most of it. Perhaps a neighbour's cat had climbed on to the roof from the old sycamore tree in the garden. Or could it be some sort of night bird? Owls? Did owls peck at the roof?

It was her last conscious thought, and Jackie slept. But next morning, the noises were still with her, in her mind and memory. She *had* heard bumping noises, and it was as though they were coming from the attic.

Jackie felt the key hanging on the chain round her neck, and was about to remove it. Then she changed her mind. She was not likely to lose it from the chain, and she felt more secure with the door locked. She let it stay there, but over breakfast she hesitated for a while, wondering whether to tell the aunts. Then she helped herself to cornflakes and listened to their usual early morning chatter. She would say nothing until she had fathomed the mystery. The noises were caused by something, and sooner or later she would find out what it had been.

* * *

Jackie worked hard on Adrian's portrait in between the times he came along to sit for her. The aunts now seemed much more settled and back to their old relationship with one another, and even as she worked, Jackie thought ahead to the time when she would go back home again.

Soon the Naismiths would all be away from Paignton, and part of her felt relieved that this should be so. She had shared Aunt Hetty's fears that Maude would be carried away by Derek

Naismith's attention to her, but now his elaborate courtesy and compliments had disappeared and he treated her with normal friendliness. It was almost as though he was leaving it to Adrian to establish special friendship with the family.

Jackie was quite pleased with her progress on the portrait, though she realised that in Adrian she had a specially good subject. He was a strange young man, she thought, as her careful brush-strokes put shadows under his chin. Sometimes he seemed to be greatly attracted to her, then he grew moody if she refused to be co-operative. She felt that there were depths to him she would not care to fathom, and she didn't want to become too involved with Adrian Naismith. She enjoyed going dancing with him, and for long walks along the sands, but she avoided being alone with him, especially at the cottage where she had felt the steely strength of his arms when he pulled her to him.

Cynthia, too, had begun to worry her, as the girl seemed to wander about aimlessly, neither joining her brother when he decided to call, nor going off on her own pursuits. Jackie would catch sight of her hanging about.

'Don't you want Cynthia to come with us?' she asked Adrian, on their way to a favourite coffee bar. 'She looks lonely somehow.'

'And play gooseberry?' he asked. 'Be your age, Jackie love. Who wants a sister hanging round one's neck?'

'I don't feel that it's all that much fun for her, that's all.'

'Her own fault. She's only good enough to look after herself, and be her own companion. That's Cynthia!'

The following afternoon Jackie was surprised when Cynthia joined her at her favourite corner of the garden where she often worked out of doors when weather permitted.

'Can I look?' she asked, 'or do artists keep portraits all covered up till they're finished?'

'I don't usually like people looking,' said Jackie, 'but so long as it's you and not Adrian. He'd probably think it was awful at this stage. I don't do my best work on portraits anyway. I doubt if I'll make my fortune painting people.'

'How will you make it?'

'Got any nice millionaires handy?' Jackie laughed. 'I doubt if I'll make it under my own steam.'

She had expected a smile at least, from the girl, but Cynthia's expression hardly changed. How sullen she can be, thought Jackie. She hardly knew what to say to the girl, and instead she moved the easel so that Cynthia could see the portrait.

The girl stared at it for a while.

'It's like him, and it isn't,' she said at last, then threw herself down on a cushion, removing her jacket and fishing in her large handbag for cigarettes.

'Smoke?'

'I don't, thank you,' Jackie told her.

She laid aside her brushes, feeling

unable to work while the other girl was near. Instead she, too, sat down on the grass and reached for a flask of coffee which Aunt Hetty had thoughtfully provided, telling her she could make her own refreshment break when she wished.

'You can have the mug, Cynthia, and I'll have the top of the flask. Okay?'

'Thanks.'

The girl took the coffee, but refused a biscuit, indicating her cigarette.

'You wouldn't be falling for him, would you?' she asked.

'Who? Adrian?'

'Who else?'

Jackie felt annoyed by the question. If she had fallen for Adrian, then Cynthia surely had no right to come butting in.

'Why?' she asked.

'Oh, no reason. Just that . . . well, he isn't so bad. You . . . er . . . could go around with someone a lot worse.'

Jackie felt surprised. The girl had spoken almost reluctantly, yet her words were an encouragement in fostering an even closer friendship with Adrian.

'I've sometimes felt you didn't care to see us go off on our own,' she said bluntly.

Cynthia's pale face flushed.

'Oh, that . . . that was nothing. I'm not very good at making friends,' she confided, and Jackie felt a pang of sympathy for her.

'Then you really must come with us,' she invited.

'No. Two's company, three's a crowd,' Cynthia informed her, 'but if you get fed up going with Adrian any time, then I wondered . . . that's why I wondered what you felt about him.'

This time Jackie could hardly conceal her surprise. Cynthia had never shown the least desire to be friendly with her before. The girl *must* be feeling a bit lost when she was asking her if they could go out on their own. Where could they possibly go which they would enjoy together?

'I'll be glad to go out with you,

Cynthia,' she said, 'if you're bored with your own company, that is. Where would you want to go?'

'Oh, we could look at clothes and things,' said Cynthia eagerly. 'I've often thought I liked what you wore, and it might suit me.'

Jackie wanted to smile. She was tall with long fair hair, whereas Cynthia was much smaller with a lighter build. Her clothes would hardly be right for the other girl.

'I can go with you if you want a second opinion when you buy something,' she offered, 'but my things would swamp you.'

Cynthia began to look sullen again.

'I was thinking about make-up, too,' she said.

'I hardly use any,' Jackie told her. 'I don't bother when I'm working, and I've left most of my stuff at home. I've got very little with me, but I don't mind looking at cosmetics with you if you're feeling flush and want to buy something.'

Cynthia said nothing for a while, but sat with her legs stretched out on the grass. She already seemed to have plenty of clothes and make-up, thought Jackie. Her handbag was capacious and seemed to be bursting at the seams, and she wore a great variety of colourful dresses and shoes. Was this some sort of effort to be friendly? Was Cynthia's manner really a cloak for extreme shyness? Up to now she would not have thought so, yet she felt as though the girl was making a real effort to be friendly, and was almost forcing herself to do so.

'I miss my record player,' said the other girl suddenly. 'I have it in my bedroom at home, and I've got heaps of records. The New Seekers, that's my favourite, even if the records are a bit old. I think they're smashing, though Adrian . . . '

She broke off abruptly.

'Doesn't he like them?' asked Jackie.

'No. He complains. He can hear them through the wall,' she said, in a rush.

'Hasn't he ever had a motor-bike?' asked Jackie. 'I had a friend whose brother complained about her watching T.V. because it was noisy, then he used to knock the windows out almost in tuning up his bike.'

Cynthia managed a smile.

'I suppose every sound is a noise to somebody.'

'Right.'

'Haven't you got a record player with you? You could probably keep it well away from your aunts, if they don't like pop.'

'No,' said Jackie, shaking her head, 'no record player either. I've never had one. I used to think I'd hate any record once I'd bought it and listened to it more than three times. It would have me screaming after that.'

Abruptly Cynthia stumbled to her feet and picked up her jacket.

'Thanks for the coffee,' she said.

'Oh . . . do you have to go yet?' asked Jackie, feeling she had not been very helpful.

'Yes.'

She grabbed the handbag, which had not been closed properly after using her lighter, and the contents spilled on to the grass.

'Damn!' said Cynthia, and Jackie laughed as she began to gather up powder compacts, hair spray, lipsticks, draw tickets and theatre programmes which looked like the collection of years, handing them to the girl to stuff back into her bag.

Her eye fell on an envelope, and she read the name, Cynthia Clarke, then it was snatched from her and she could see anger sparking in the other girl's eyes.

'I can do it,' said Cynthia. 'I just forgot my bag was unshut.'

She fumbled with the catch, then swung away without another word, almost running in her haste, and Jackie was left feeling oddly upset. There was something here she just did not understand. Why Cynthia Clarke? She brooded on it as she cleaned her brushes, feeling that work had been ruined for the day. Then she remembered the thin white mark on Cynthia's finger which Aunt Hetty had taken to be a broken engagement.

Only it was not a broken engagement, thought Jackie, as understanding dawned. It was a broken marriage. Yet why had not Adrian or Derek Naismith introduced the girl as Cynthia Clarke, and not Naismith? Had there been a divorce? And had Cynthia come back to her old home, and tried to forget that she had ever been married?

Jackie decided to say nothing about it. It was none of her business, and in another week they would all be gone. It would only give Aunt Hetty more cause for speculation, and would maybe make for dissension again between the aunts.

Slowly she walked indoors, remembering the anger and, perhaps, a touch of fear on the other girl's face. She felt sympathy for Cynthia, remembering her remarks that her boy-friend would come crawling back, something he always did. Could she be expecting that to happen, and was she lost and upset because it hadn't?

Jackie had a sudden vision of the girl hanging about on the fringe while she went out with Adrian, and Cynthia's loneliness caught at her. The girl was sullen and inscrutable, and she didn't really like her, but she would try to do better, vowed Jackie. She would try to be more of a friend for Cynthia for the rest of their holiday.

Aunt Hetty was just putting down the telephone when Jackie went into the house, and she turned to the girl with a pleased smile.

'Oh, I was just going to come and look for you, dear, but the young man said you mustn't be disturbed. He knows about artists.'

'What young man?' asked Jackie.

Adrian wasn't usually so considerate.

'Your friend from home. Jonathan . . . er . . . Nelson? Didn't we meet his parents one time when we visited the cottage?'

'Jonathan!'

Jackie's disappointment was intense. While she had been in the garden coping with Cynthia, Jonathan had been on the telephone!

'Oh, Aunt Hetty! I'd have liked to talk to him. And I was just packing up my stuff, too!'

'It's all right, darling. He's coming here this evening. He's booked into a hotel along the sea front at Paignton and I've invited him to join us for an evening meal. Don't you think that was a good idea?'

Jackie's heart seemed to miss a beat, then race like mad. Jonathan was coming to visit them this evening! Her hands flew to her hair, and she looked down at her grubby jeans.

'Oh, goodness, Aunt Hetty! I'd better have a bath and change.'

'That's right, dear. I'll go and have a word with Maude over what we should serve up. It's nice for you to have your own friends here.'

Jackie had changed into a print dress

in delicate pastel shades, with a demure white collar, and was combing out her freshly washed hair when the doorbell rang. She had intended to watch out for Jonathan, but she was too late.

She looked at herself critically in the mirror feeling that she looked like a schoolgirl beside the lovely, sophisticated Janetta Hodge, but she still thought she had made the right decision to be just herself, and not make any special effort to dress up even more. Her skin glowed like a peach now that it had been touched with the warm sunshine, and her fair hair had silvery glints.

As she walked downstairs, Aunt Maude had gone to open the door to Jonathan, but it was Adrian Naismith who stood there, looking smart in his dark suit and the cream silk shirt he loved to wear. His eyes lit up when he saw Jackie.

'Hello, love. On time for once! It isn't often you're ready so promptly.'

Jackie stared.

'What . . . what do you mean, Adrian? I . . . I wasn't expecting you.'

This time it was Adrian who looked taken aback.

'Dinner, then dancing, darling. You *can't* have forgotten! I said either Kent's Cavern this afternoon or dancing tonight. You chose dancing, so I took Cyn out to lunch. She seemed a bit down and hardly ate anything. I thought I would give her an appetite.'

Jackie swallowed. *Had* she made such an arrangement? She had no recollection of it. The aunts had come out to join her in the hall, looking at her questioningly.

But she just *couldn't* go off with Adrian now that Jonathan was coming. Yet here he was, all set and eagerly awaiting a night out. How *could* she have forgotten!

Mention of Cynthia, too, had reminded her of her inward promises to try to help the girl.

'Can't you take Cynthia again?' she asked.

Jackie's cheeks flamed. It was almost as though he were setting out to give Jonathan quite the wrong impression. She saw Aunt Maude looking at her reproachfully, no doubt longing to tell her off for wanting to back out of arrangements when something better turned up. She was a stickler for keeping promises. Or was it for some other reason?

Aunt Hetty, on the other hand, looked annoyed. She didn't like Adrian and was only tolerating him because it was temporary, but if she could have seen the last of him now, then she would have waved him goodbye with pleasure. No doubt she was counting on Jonathan to get rid of him somehow.

Yet the sick feeling of disappointment was welling up in Jackie. She had felt excited and keyed up at the thought of seeing Jonathan again. Was he here on his own? she wondered. He must be, or he would not have accepted an invitation without mentioning that he had a friend, even if it was Janetta Hodge. Was he still seeing her a lot?

But now everything was in ashes as she went to get her coat. At least she knew, now, that Adrian bored her and she regretted ever letting any friendship develop between them.

She should never have encouraged him, though he had not needed much encouragement. None of them had. They had seemed to cling round Maidenbank like flies attracted to a honeypot, as though they all wanted to recapture the times they had spent there.

It would have been better if the aunts had changed everything, all the furniture, decorating and garden, then it would not have seemed like the same house, and would not have evoked old memories.

Then people like the Naismiths would have stayed away, and she would not be in this position now.

With flags of colour in her cheeks, she returned to the hall where Aunt

Hetty had taken Jonathan's coat.

'I . . . I'm sorry to leave you like this,' she managed.

'That's all right. I mustn't keep you from . . .' he glanced at Adrian, ' . . . from more pressing matters. Have a good time.'

Again he glanced at Adrian and Jackie saw a sudden flash in his eyes, as his fingers tightened on her and he placed his hands on her shoulders and kissed her firmly.

'Goodnight, my sweet, in case I don't see you when you get back.'

Adrian's face had darkened, but when Jackie again looked at Jonathan, she could see no real warmth in his returning glance. In fact, there were old telltale signs that he was furiously angry.

Then in a moment she and Adrian were out in the garden, the door shut behind them.

'I *don't* remember saying I'd go dancing with you, Adrian,' she said furiously. 'I really don't. Yet you put me in such a position, I couldn't get out of it.'

This time it was his fingers which felt steely on her arm.

'Don't you, Jackie darling? Oh, but I'm sure you did. I told Aunt Maude you had when I rang this evening and she was all excited over your friend's arrival. Just ask her. Anyway, we're off to enjoy ourselves, aren't we? I thought we would both have been bored if I'd accepted Aunt Hetty's offer to stay for dinner. I intend you to forget old boy-friends, my love,' he said softly. 'I only want you to think about *me*.'

'That's impossible, Adrian. I don't love you, and . . . and I've known Jonathan Nelson all my life.'

'The boy next door! Nobody ends up with the boy next door, love. Not nowadays. You'd know all there was to know about him, and there would be no surprises. Think how dull that would be.'

Jackie could not have agreed less. She was feeling, more and more, that

Jonathan was becoming a stranger to her, and she was half afraid of the anger she had felt in him when she walked out with Adrian.

Yet she didn't know Adrian either! Nor did she want to. Sometimes she still felt that he repelled her in spite of his looks and the admiring glances cast at both of them when they were out together, he being as dark as she was fair.

But in spite of the good dinner, and the dancing, Jackie could feel no uplift of spirit and as they walked home in the clear fresh air, tanged with the sea, she pushed Adrian away as he held her closely and insisted on kissing her.

'It's no good, Adrian.'

'You can't get rid of me so easily, Jackie,' he said in a soft voice. 'I'm fine to have around when there's no one else, but as soon as a boy-friend turns up, old Adrian gets shown the door. Well, you can forget that, darling. I still intend to enjoy the rest of my holiday, and to have you help in doing it. Aren't you painting my portrait after all?'

'I can send it on to you!'

'Didn't you say you'd need another sitting tomorrow?'

She *had* said that.

'Well, I'll be around at the usual time in the afternoon. Your friend seems to have gone. No doubt bored by the two old ladies.'

'They aren't boring.'

'A matter of opinion. They bore me, but then, so does Father. *And* Cynthia, at times. But I find you a lot of fun, especially when you try to cut and run. You'd regret that, if I just let you, then you would want me back, so I'm doing you a favour by hanging on, darling. I really am.'

'Oh, go away, Adrian!' she cried, 'and don't come back. If I don't bore you, then you bore me!'

Again she could feel the steel in his fingers on her arm.

'Till tomorrow afternoon, Jackie. Goodnight, darling.'

He turned away and she let herself

154

into Maidenbank with the key her aunts had had cut for her. The house was in darkness, but as she switched on the kitchen light, she saw a small note which told her she could have hot chocolate, and that Jonathan had stayed quite late.

Rather tiredly Jackie climbed the stairs to bed.

6

Jackie was up before the aunts the following morning. She had slept badly and had awakened early with the sudden nervous fear of the attic which could come back to haunt her at times. The noises she had heard had not been repeated, and gradually she realised that they were probably caused by birds, or even a cat who had been chased up there by a dog. Cats had been known to climb pretty high in their fear.

Nevertheless she had kept the attic key on the chain she always wore, and she was happier to let it stay there until she said goodbye to Goodrington and returned home.

'You *are* early, dear,' said Aunt Hetty, when she appeared a short time later.

'So are you,' smiled Jackie.

'Old habits. I can't lie abed too long.

Are you having coffee as usual?'

'Mm,' Jackie nodded absently.

'Then I'll make tea for Maude and me. Did you enjoy your evening?'

'It was all right.'

'Young Mr Nelson was very charming. He entertained Maude and me all evening with stories relating to his work. I never realised there were so many pitfalls in architecture. I've heard about people designing their own house and forgetting the stairs, but Mr Nelson says it *can* happen, then an architect gets called in to correct the mistake. Oh, he had us both amused, I can tell you. It was such a change from that Derek Naismith. Did you know he turned up, too, and smarmed all over Maude as usual? I was afraid young Jonathan would get bored and leave, but he seemed to find Naismith very interesting, and stayed until he left. Maybe he was hoping you'd be home, dear, before he had to go.'

'I doubt it,' said Jackie, rather bitterly. 'Is he coming back today?'

'He didn't say. Ah, here's Maude. I've made us a pot of tea. I was telling Jackie about Derek Naismith turning up.'

'To your annoyance,' said Maude, rather tartly. She didn't look her best either.

'Certainly. He's an objectionable man.'

'Only to you. And anyway, there'll be no need to worry about him longer than Saturday of this week. They're going.'

'Going?' cried Jackie, and was amazed at the relief which swept over her. She had been getting a 'thing' about these people, she told herself. She had been feeling as though she'd never be free of them, but it was that simple really. She had only to be polite this week, then have them away for evermore. Being downright rude seemed to have had no effect, but soon it would no longer be necessary.

And Jonathan was in Paignton! She knew the charming white-painted hotel where he was staying very well. Should she telephone, or go along and see him?

But Adrian was turning up for another sitting. Jackie had felt annoyed about that, wishing fervently that she had never started the picture, and determined to work on it feverishly, if necessary, so that she could give it to Adrian with instructions for varnishing and framing.

She left the breakfast table with a lightened heart, and towards mid-morning she decided to ring up the hotel, longing to speak to Jonathan again. But he was out, she was told, and the receptionist had no idea when he would return.

Rather despondently Jackie put the receiver back, then returned to her painting, trying to work with concentration. Of course Jonathan was likely to be out. He would not be sitting around in a hotel all day long.

It seemed hours later when Aunt Hetty suddenly exclaimed that she could see him approaching the gate, then made a curious sort of exclamation as she went towards the door. Jackie looked out of the window, but could see nothing, then as the door opened, she understood Aunt Hetty's odd little noise. Jonathan was ushering in Cynthia.

'We met walking up,' he explained cheerfully. 'It seems I've met the whole family now.'

'Oh, how . . . how nice,' said Aunt Hetty, looking at Cynthia rather frostily. 'Do come in, both of you.'

'I was coming to see Jackie,' said Cynthia, 'to ask her if she could come shopping with me. But it doesn't matter now.'

'Oh no, I mustn't be allowed to interfere with plans,' Jonathan said. 'I didn't expect Jackie to be free all day and every day, when I suddenly descended on her.'

But Jackie was in no mood to be co-operative this time. First Adrian, and now Cynthia! But this time she was not going to be caught.

'I had no arrangement,' she began, 'so I'm quite free . . . '

'Oh, but I insist!' said Jonathan, his eyes gleaming. 'You mustn't change plans for me, as I've already told you. Cynthia would be very disappointed if you spoiled her arrangements, Jackie, and her holiday is nearly at an end. No doubt you want to shop for gifts? A second opinion is always helpful.'

'Yes, it is,' said Cynthia, looking at Jonathan rather uneasily.

Jackie was growing even more angry. If Jonathan really wanted to see her, he would not be pushing her into arrangements for going out with other people. Surely he would want her to himself, even for a little while!

Yet he seemed in no hurry to see her on her own. Why had he come, then? Had he been granted an extra week's holiday or something, and had come down to keep an eye on her? Was Janet feeling concerned about her? Yet she had always written home, and she hadn't gone into many details about

161

the Naismiths . . . not enough to cause her mother any anxiety. She had never written glowingly about Adrian.

'How long are you here?' she asked him.

'That depends,' he said carefully, and glanced at Cynthia, who turned to stare at him.

'On what?'

'Oh, various things . . . amusement, places to visit . . . the weather! I have no cut and dried plans. Can I see what you're doing, Jackie?'

She flushed as Jonathan studied Adrian's portrait with concentration, while Cynthia stood around aimlessly till Jackie asked her, rather impatiently, to sit down.

'Mhm. Very nice,' he agreed. 'Don't you think so, Cynthia? Very good of your brother.'

Again his eyes glittered a little as he turned to Jackie.

'So you haven't been wasting your time since you came.'

There were two ways of taking that,

but she chose to accept the innocent interpretation.

'No. I've been painting every day. It isn't so much fun now. Adrian is paying me to paint his portrait.'

'A good arrangement. You've still got quite a lot to do.'

'I'm working on it.'

'Then it's unfair of us to steal your time.' He turned to Cynthia with a smile. 'I tell you what, can't I take Jackie's place and advise you over purchases? I'm a very good second opinion. We can leave Jackie free to get on with her work.'

Jackie managed to stifle her frustration and anger, as Cynthia first of all looked uncertain, then shrugged a little.

'That's kind of you. I . . . er . . . I was a bit at a loose end. I don't really have much shopping to do.'

'Then why don't we go and see the sights? The tropical fish, for example. I'm interested in odd fish . . . aren't you?'

Cynthia was looking at him rather distrustfully.

'I . . . I don't know.'

'Then let's go and find out. I'll see you again when you're free, Jackie.'

Angry and frustrated, she looked at Jonathan's hand holding Cynthia's arm.

'So Miss Hodge isn't here with you, then?'

His eyebrows rose.

'Who would look after the office? Of course she decided to stay in Bath.'

'No doubt it isn't extravagant enough for her.'

Jackie knew she was behaving badly, but she felt raw with disappointment.

'I wonder what caused that remark,' Jonathan was saying softly.

Then Aunt Maude came through to offer refreshments.

'No, we're just going, I'm afraid,' Jonathan apologised. 'We mustn't keep Jackie from her work. Cheerio, and I'll see you another time. Come on, Cynthia.'

She hated Jonathan, thought Jackie

rebelliously, as they left the house. How *could* he go off with Cynthia like that, when he must know she wanted to talk to him, and that her heart felt sore and empty without him? She wanted to cry instead of to paint, but instead she jabbed some paint on to her palette and mixed it carefully, trying her best to concentrate.

She did not want to stay on here at Goodrington now the aunts seemed so much more settled. Yet she didn't want to go home either, especially with Jonathan so near, and with so much power to torment her.

The future seemed dark with shadows, and she couldn't see the way. Could she go back to London? She had been happy there, as had her father, and she had a sudden longing for the old days and her home there. She and her father had both loved it so much.

But now there seemed to be little hope of having her own home. The cottage was lovely, but it was all Janet's. Jackie began to feel even more lonely than she had ever done in her life.

Her heart was sore, when Adrian finally arrived for a sitting, looking fit and energetic. He had spent the morning swimming, he told her.

'Doesn't Cynthia share your pleasure in swimming?' she asked, rather tartly. 'She came looking for me, and has gone off with Jonathan. He wanted her to go with him.'

Adrian frowned.

'Who is this Jonathan Nelson?' he asked. 'What does he do?'

But Jackie didn't want to discuss Jonathan, especially not with Adrian.

'He's a friend . . . of the family,' she said flatly. 'As to what he does and all that, I'm sure he'll tell you all about it if you ask him.'

'You aren't in a good mood today,' he accused her. 'Surely it's natural for me to wonder about the man if he's taking my sister out?'

'You've no need to fear,' she said tiredly. 'He's a solid citizen. She'll be well looked after by Jonathan Nelson.'

'He sounds like a pillar of society. A lawyer? Policeman?'

'You'll have to look at his feet,' she said, laughing, and decided to change the subject. She wanted to keep all thoughts of Jonathan to herself.

'Can you sit over there and turn your head a little, Adrian? Watch my pencil. Hold it!'

She worked quickly, but he seemed restless and nervous, or it could be that he was now finding boredom in posing for a portrait.

'You've moved!' she accused.

'Can't we leave it, for heaven's sake? Never mind the beastly picture.'

'You wanted it! Are you changing your mind now?'

'Oh, I don't know. No, of course not. I'll still have it.'

'You needn't,' she said proudly. 'I can always use the canvas again.'

'Oh, don't be so huffy,' he said. 'Your boy-friend has upset me rather muscling in like this. All of a sudden I'm jealous, Jackie.'

167

She shrugged. 'I'm trying to forget Jonathan. He goes his own way.'

'Why did he turn up here, just like that? Did you know he was coming?'

'No, I didn't. Though if you ask me, Mother wants to keep an eye on me.'

'Why?'

Adrian's eyes were suddenly shrewd.

'What have you told her about me?'

'Nothing . . . much. Just little things in letters. Don't worry, she isn't having you looked over. She knows we're just friends . . . or should I say business friends, since I'm working on your behalf at the moment?'

He rose from his chair and came over to stand beside her.

'Jackie!' he said urgently. 'Jackie . . . Oh, damn!'

The front door opened and Maude came in, carrying a shopping bag. They could hear her voice in the hall, then Hetty's lighter tones in reply.

'Talk about chaperones!' said Adrian savagely. 'If I took you in my arms, they would only stand around and watch! Couldn't you have sent one of them with Cynthia? Can I never talk to you on your own in this house? Don't they ever go off for the day with the Mothers' Union or something?'

Jackie was laughing.

'Hardly. It's their house, Adrian, after all.'

'Yes. Worse luck!'

The tone was bitter and she drew back, her eyes sobering. Adrian had sounded as though he really grudged the aunts this house. Had it *really* been so special? It was an attractive house, but no better than many others of the same size.

And from what she had seen of the Naismiths, they didn't seem all that poor! Surely their home in Liverpool must be a nice one?

'You couldn't have bought it, could you? I mean, it wouldn't be practical for you to move here.'

'We weren't given the chance,' said Adrian. 'Were we?'

'*Would* you have wanted it?'

He turned to look at her, his dark eyes brooding, then he smiled with one of his quick changes of mood.

'Only if you go with it, my love.'

'Well, I don't.' She matched her tone to his.

'Here come some more old dears . . .'

'The aunts are having friends in today, people they knew when they kept the boarding house.'

Adrian made a face.

'It's like a vicarage tea party! I'm off. Look, Jackie . . . I must see you here on your own before I go. I want to . . . talk a little.'

She went with him to the door, but didn't offer any suggestions. She did not particularly want to hear what Adrian had to say, especially when he was beginning to make it clear that it might be a talk on their future. She had tried to tell him they had no future together, but obviously he thought he would be able to persuade her.

'Cheerio, Adrian.'

'Cheerio, darling. See you soon.'

Slowly she went back to the portrait and stared at it moodily. It wasn't as good as she had hoped. There had been far too many upsets and interruptions. But her self-discipline insisted that she finish it. At least she had corrected the jawline which was heavier than she had imagined. And the mouth a trifle thinner. Adrian wasn't quite so handsome when one got used to him, she thought dispassionately.

But Jonathan had a face which grew more attractive all the time. Had Cynthia enjoyed his company?

'Are you alone, dear?' asked Aunt Hetty. 'Wouldn't you like to come through and have tea with us?'

Jackie shook her head, then changed her mind when she saw Hetty was disappointed.

'All right. Thanks, Aunt Hetty.'

Maybe she was destined to be on her own most of her life, thought Jackie. Like a great many other ladies. She would have to learn to be self-reliant, that's what, as some of their guests were. She looked round them with respect.

★ ★ ★

It was Cynthia's turn to call round the following morning and try to pump Jackie about Jonathan, though by now Jackie's disappointment in the way things were turning out was making her feel cross and unco-operative. She was working hard on the last of the portrait, to give it a day or two to dry before it was comparatively safe for Adrian to take home.

'It will need to dry over a long period . . . six months, if possible,' she had told Adrian, at one sitting, 'then you can varnish it and have it framed.' An imp of mischief showed in her eyes. 'Perhaps I'll be able to come to the ancestral home and see it hung.'

Adrian looked taken aback, but he quickly recovered.

'Why not, love? We'll have to arrange it before I leave for the old grindstone

172

again.' He sighed deeply. 'Too bad we can't all carry our jobs around with us, and do it just where the mood takes us, but I'd have quite a task trotting a printing machine around.'

'What do you print?' she asked, interested. Adrian had never really discussed his work. 'Booklets? Pamphlets? Leaflets?'

'Mainly small stuff. Billheads, tickets and . . . '

'Wedding invitations?'

'Yes. That would be one advantage in marrying a printer. The wedding invitations would be free.'

She liked him in this bantering mood, and sometimes she wondered if he would be a happier person away from his family. Sometimes she felt that they all had an adverse effect on one another, yet they all stuck together. She could imagine they would be a close-knit group when his mother was alive.

'Tell me about your mother,' she invited, 'and about what you do at home.'

'Now you want me to bore you,' he evaded. 'Why do you think we get away for a holiday? There's nothing attractive about our old printing presses. I assure you. I'd rather talk about you!'

Though now it seemed that Cynthia would rather talk about Jonathan, thought Jackie, as she sat cross-legged on the grass, the inevitable handbag beside her, though Jackie noticed that it bulged a great deal less. No doubt she had decided to reduce the contents to avoid embarrassment in future.

'Have you known him long?' Cynthia was asking.

'Longer than Adrian,' Jackie prevaricated. 'Didn't Jon tell you?'

'He clammed up on me every time. I tried to find out about *him*. He said he only wanted to talk about *me*.'

'Oh, did you?' thought Jackie, scowling away as she jabbed in more paint. Jealousy was giving her a raw taste in her mouth. Well, if Cynthia wanted information, she wasn't getting it out of her. How nosy the Naismiths were!

'Does he live in your village? Where is it again . . . Chip . . . '

'Chipping Sodbury. No, he doesn't.'

'Oh.' Cynthia was beginning to look sulky again. 'Is he . . . is he in business there, then? Or a solicitor, maybe?'

Jonathan must look as though he knew a lot about the law, thought Jackie.

'Are you seeing him again?' she asked.

'He says so.'

'Well, I've no doubt he'll be telling you all about himself, though I was just wondering why you're so interested.'

Cynthia smiled.

'Why is any girl interested in a man?'

'Because she finds him attractive. Though I thought you already had . . . someone special.'

Cynthia coloured, allowing her hair to fall forward on to her face. Jackie suddenly felt mean, and rather sorry for the girl. Again she felt that she was troubled about something, and she wondered if she ought to ask her straight out about it, and offer to help. Where was the unknown Mr Clarke? Was he in Liverpool? Or had he left Cynthia there before they came away on holiday? Was she, perhaps, hoping to see him *here*, in Torbay?

Suddenly the point of Cynthia's questions . . . and Adrian's too, for that matter . . . began to dawn on Jackie. Some people were rather reluctant to consult a solicitor, if it was someone unknown to them. It was almost like stepping into an alien world. Perhaps Cynthia needed the advice of a solicitor rather badly, and she was hoping that Jonathan might fit the bill, since he looked like a professional man.

But the chances of him being connected with the law were very remote, she reminded herself. They were being hopeful! Though, of course, they were no worse off, but if Jonathan *could* have helped them, they might have been better off.

'Are you troubled about something, Cynthia?' she asked, and walked over to the other girl. She was unprepared for the way she shot to her feet.

'Whatever gave you that idea?'

'Just that you *look* anxious at times. Then asking if Jonathan was a solicitor. Do you need a solicitor's help?'

'Honestly!' cried Cynthia, backing away, 'you don't half get hold of the wrong end of the stick. What would I need a solicitor for?'

'I saw a ring mark on your finger when you first came. I . . . I wondered if . . . if you'd been married and it had broken down.'

Cynthia's face went pale.

'Why should I tell you? My affairs are my own, so keep your nose out of it. I'm going home soon so . . . so just leave me alone!'

She turned to go.

'I'm sorry,' said Jackie sincerely. 'I didn't mean to pry into your private affairs. I don't care in the least whether you've been married, engaged or . . . or anything.'

'Then shut up about it!'

Cynthia stumped away, then she stopped and came back hesitantly.

'Just forget it . . . will you? Forget we even talked about it, and for heaven's sake, don't tell Adrian!'

'No, of course not,' Jackie agreed.

Though she was very thoughtful as Cynthia swung away. Surely the girl could not have been married without her family knowing! She had obviously been wearing a ring, though of course, it could have been an engagement ring.

Jackie shrugged as she packed her things. Why bother anyway? She would do exactly as Cynthia had asked. She would forget all about it.

7

The following afternoon Jonathan rang before lunch, and asked to speak to Jackie. Aunt Maude came to find her.

Aunt Maude had been rather quiet over the past day or two, as though she had something on her mind, and more than once Jackie wondered whether she ought to tackle her about it, but she had left it to Hetty, who was good at knowing when her sister was worried, and also good at helping to put things right.

Now she greeted Jackie with a smile.

'Your Mr Nelson, dear. On the phone.'

'He isn't *my* Mr Nelson, Aunt Maude.'

'Well, you're the one he knows. He asks to speak to you.'

'Good of him, considering he's practically ignored me since he came.'

'I think he's jealous of Adrian, dear. I think he was put out when he found you going about with another young man. But old friends are best, you know, Jackie. We don't really know the Naismiths, do we?'

This was spoken rather frostily, and Jackie glanced speculatively at Aunt Maude as she went to the telephone. Was she feeling put out over Derek Naismith, whose visits had been decidedly fewer since the other two came on the scene?

Jackie picked up the telephone.

'Jonathan?'

'Hello, Jackie. Look, can you meet me for lunch? I thought we could have it here at my hotel, then we could sit in the lounge, or go out into the gardens for half an hour. It's quiet here today. We can sit and contemplate the ducks and ducklings.'

She could hear the teasing note in his voice.

'How delightful! Unfortunately I'm engaged for lunch.'

'Who with? Not with the Naismiths, anyway. I've managed to check up and they all seem to be having a day out together at Babbacombe. Doing their sightseeing now they're going home on Saturday.'

'Why should it matter to you who I'm lunching with?' she asked angrily. 'You probably only want me because you can't have Janetta or Cynthia.'

'Look, Jackie, forget Janetta and Cynthia,' said Jonathan urgently. 'Can you be here at one o'clock? I want to talk to you. About your aunts, as a matter of fact . . . '

'The aunts?' Illogically she felt disappointed again, and she wanted to shout at him, that she never wanted to see him again! Why did she have to fall in love with him like this, and give him the power to hurt her?

Always, secretly, she had been hopeful that he would come to care for her, too, and show his determination to win her, overcoming all obstacles. But instead he made no objections when

181

she was going out with someone else, and even now when he was so insistent that she lunch with him, it was not for her own sake, but because he wanted to talk about the aunts!

'What about them?' she asked.

'I'll tell you when I see you. Ask them to excuse you for lunch, there's a good girl, and come over here for one o'clock. I'll arrange it from this end, and I'll keep a lookout for you in the lounge. I'll be doing the *Times* crossword.' There was a short silence, then he said gently, 'Do come, Jackie. It's important. I would come and fetch you, only I'm waiting for a telephone call.'

'Oh, all right.'

She hung up the receiver, then anger boiled again as she remembered how he had told her to get the aunts to excuse her for lunch. How did he know that her luncheon date was here at Maidenbank?

'He's got a nerve!' she said, aloud, and Aunt Maude paused on her way to help Hetty in the kitchen.

'What's that, Jackie?'

'Oh, nothing, darling. I was just thinking of Jonathan Nelson. He wants me to have lunch with him at his hotel today.'

'Well, how nice! Just leave everything, and go up to get changed. I thought he'd be inviting you to do something nice very soon.'

'I don't feel in the mood to go,' said Jackie.

'Oh, but you'll enjoy it when you get there. If the other young man comes . . . Adrian . . . I shall tell him you're otherwise engaged. If you ask me, he takes you far too much for granted!'

Jackie had been feeling the same thing about Jonathan! She hated being taken for granted.

'Will you be glad to see the last of the Naismiths, Aunt Maude?' she asked curiously. 'I thought it was Aunt Hetty who couldn't stand them.'

'They . . . they're unreliable,' said Aunt Maude. Hetty came through with a tray of cutlery and glasses.

'Oh, Aunt Hetty, I'm sorry, I've just been invited out to lunch by Jonathan Nelson. I . . . I wish I'd said I wouldn't go.'

'You're like other women before you,' said Hetty, rather disagreeably. 'All ready to rush off when the finger beckons.'

'Jackie isn't like that,' Maude defended. 'She had to be persuaded.'

'While your ears flapped listening.'

'The telephone in this house is far from private. You must have heard it, too, if you were honest enough to admit it.'

'I . . . I'll just run upstairs and change,' said Jackie hurriedly. 'Er . . . I hope you can both eat a little more . . . '

'It's chops,' said Hetty. 'You must show me how to divide your chop between Maude and me.'

'I'm quite sure *you'll* be able to eat two,' said Maude. 'You know one is quite enough for me.'

'Scraggy. That's what you are,' said Hetty.

'Oh, you two!' cried Jackie. 'What's happened to you both? You're back at the bickering stage again. I thought I was helping a bit by just *being* here, but you're as bad as ever.'

'Sorry,' said Hetty, rather gruffly. 'I got a bad sleep last night, that's all.'

'Were you worried about anything?'

She saw the aunts glance at one another.

'Not specially, no.'

'Maybe it's me, then,' said Jackie. 'Maybe I've been here long enough.'

Had she outstayed her welcome? she wondered. Maybe that was what Jonathan wanted to talk to her about. Maybe he could see that the aunts were fed up having her, only she was too closely concerned to see it for herself.

But they were both protesting, almost with alarm.

'No, dear, please don't go just yet. Why, the summer won't be over for at least another five weeks.'

'You'll have plenty of work to do after that portrait,' said Maude. 'Do your seascapes again. I don't really like the portrait.'

'Isn't it a good likeness?' asked Jackie, disappointed.

'Oh, it's an *excellent* likeness. That's just it. That young man is very good-looking. He's just like some of those very handsome young film stars we used to have in the thirties, and I expect him to produce a tall hat and cane from somewhere and start dancing every time I see that picture.'

'Oh, Aunt Maude!'

Jackie burst out laughing and soon the other two were joining in, and with relief she saw that their ill-humour with one another had passed.

'Sorry about lunch,' she apologised gently.

'That's all right, dear. I'm too old a hand to be put out with cancelled meals. Have a good time. I like your young man.'

'He's *not* my young man,' said Jackie automatically.

She took extra care over her appearance, however, pleased that the fresh sea air and sunshine had made her skin glow with the radiance of youth and health.

Then she got out her small car. It wasn't far, but she wanted to be sure of arriving in bandbox condition.

Why had Jonathan wanted to see her about the aunts? she wondered. If he wanted her to go back to Chipping Sodbury, when his holiday was finished, and leave them, then he was in for a disappointment. She had promised to stay on for an indefinite period. They were both so keen to have her stay.

Jackie parked the car in the hotel car park, then pushed open a small wrought-iron gate and mounted the steps to the hotel entrance, walking straight through to the lounge. There was no sign of Jonathan, and she looked about feeling a little bit lost. He had promised to look out for her.

Then a hand took her elbow and she looked round, nervous excitement washing over her as her eyes met his. The inward joy at being with him again made her tremble, even as they walked over to a small table.

'We have ten minutes before lunch,' said Jonathan, looking at his watch. 'What will you have, Jackie?'

'Nothing, thanks. I . . . I don't feel I . . . I want anything.'

'A poor lookout for our meal.'

Again his eyes were laughing, and she began to feel annoyed all over again. He had been here for several days, and this was the first time he had even tried to see her on her own. Yet not so long ago he had asked her to marry him. It was obvious now that it had not been because he was in love with her. He might even have been trying to use her to placate his father. She had felt dissension between Jon and his parents that night she had delivered the picture.

'How are your mother and father,

Jonathan?' she asked evenly. 'Have you finished all your alterations . . . or was it improvements? . . . to Merton Lodge?'

'Both,' he said blandly, 'and decorations. It looks like a respectable home now.'

'Are your parents pleased with it?'

'You must ask them,' he said softly, and she flushed. It was really none of her business, but she was having to remind herself that the Jonathan who was beside her now, looking dear and familiar, was the same Jonathan who lived extravagantly, and entertained lavishly when she suspected his parents could not really afford it. He obviously had little consideration for them, she reminded herself, and none at all for her!

'Anyway, let's not discuss Merton Lodge,' he said, taking her hand. 'I want to talk about you.'

'About the aunts,' she reminded him.

'You and the aunts. You look wonderful, Jackie. Did I tell you?'

The ready colour rose in her cheeks,

and angrily she felt tears sting her eyes. She was saved from replying by having to go into the dining-room, which was fairly quiet.

'My table is over in the corner, near the window,' said Jonathan, leading the way.

'What about the aunts?' asked Jackie, when they had finally decided on their order.

'I like them both. I enjoyed talking to them that first night when you walked out on me.'

'You urged me to go.'

'Well, my love, a date's a date. I can't allow you to go back on your word for me. For all I know, you could have been hating me for butting in.'

'I told you, I hadn't made any arrangements.'

Suddenly his tone changed and he reached for her hand.

'I'm glad, Jackie,' he said quietly. 'I would like your assurance that that fellow, Adrian Naismith, doesn't mean anything to you . . . that you haven't fallen in love with him.'

She pulled her hand away, angry spots of colour in her cheeks. He would like her assurance! He obviously did not care a hoot about her, but he didn't want her to be interested in anyone else.

'Talk about dog-in-the-manger,' she said, 'that about takes the biscuit! *You* don't want me, but if someone else shows interest, I'm supposed to . . . to . . . '

'Stop shouting! People are looking,' said Jonathan calmly. 'Eat your melon and calm down.'

'You make me very angry, Jonathan.'

'That's obvious. I never realised you were such a firebrand. I always thought you were a nice quiet ordinary girl . . . '

'Who would agree to every suggestion you make, and who would hang on to your every word. Not a chance, Jonathan.'

He was grinning again.

'What have you really got to know

about these people, Jackie? Cross my heart, I have a reason for asking.'

'They're business people from Liverpool. Printers in a small way.'

'*Genuine* printers?'

'What do you mean *genuine* printers?'

'I mean, not stationers who farm out printing orders to someone else. They do their own printing?'

'Of course. Adrian knows quite a lot about printing. I've learned a little about it as part of my art course, and we've talked of silk screen work, engraving, all that sort of thing. He's no charlatan, Jon, if that's what you're thinking. These are genuine people.'

'The father, too? Does he do actual printing?'

'Of course. What *is* all this? The daughter helps on the business side, something her mother used to do. Only she died a short time ago, and I rather think she was the mainstay of the family. Mr Naismith went to pieces, rather, and had to come down to

Goodrington to get away from it all. That's why he hung around Maidenbank. They used to rent it in the summer months.'

'So did other people, I believe. A cottage kept for summer letting . . . '

'That's right. But the others didn't have a tragic loss like he did. It was sheer nostalgia which kept him hanging around, combined with the fact that his wife had looked like a younger edition of Aunt Maude. I rather think he mooned around a bit, looking at her and wanting to be with her. It got Aunt Hetty all steamed up.'

'Hm.' Jonathan had ordered steak and now he attacked it vigorously. 'And who is looking after the business now that the whole family have arrived?'

'I don't know. Don't they have holiday times in some towns and cities? Like the Glasgow Fair in July? Perhaps everywhere is closed this fortnight.'

'Perhaps.'

She looked at him, seeing the look of worry in his eyes, and gradually she realised that Jonathan really was concerned.

Then she was remembering her own concern when she first came to Goodrington. The aunts had seemed very uneasy and unsettled. Could it be that they had mentioned anything about this to Jonathan? She had dismissed it all as a differing opinion between them over Derek Naismith.

'They aren't still worried over Mr Naismith, are they?' she asked. 'I mean, were they telling you things that evening, Jonathan?'

'What sort of things?'

'Oh, I dunno. They were a little bit at odds with one another when I arrived, but they seemed to get over it.'

'Hm,' said Jonathan again.

She offered him more vegetables, but he shook his head, as though he was beginning to lose his appetite.

'Don't you feel something odd about it all, Jackie? Something wrong?'

'In what way?'

'In the whole set-up. Your aunts buy a

house, then they begin to get pestered by a previous tenant, with glib excuses all laid on. Soon the whole family descends. Father, perhaps, hasn't made as much progress as he likes with Aunt Maude, owing to Hetty's disapproval, and now a third member of the family turns up and takes up residence. You. So son Adrian comes on the scene and makes a play for you, and just for good measure, daughter Cynthia hangs about. If Jackie isn't susceptible to Adrian's charms, then she might react to having a girl-friend around. They can either be 'girls together' or Cynthia can look all pathetic and get sympathy out of Jackie. Is she a poor lonely little girl whom nobody loves?'

She stared at him, hardly knowing what to say.

'Because you can take it from me, she's no such thing. Ability to take care of herself is well up her list of accomplishments.'

'Maybe there are things you don't know, Jonathan. Maybe she's not so self-sufficient as you make out.'

'What makes you say that?'

She wondered if she should tell him about the bag and the envelope which she had picked up with the other things. Cynthia Clarke. Somewhere the girl had experienced trouble and unhappiness. Jackie remembered her small slight figure and the droop to her shoulders. No, she could not go gossiping about her to Jonathan.

'Just . . . various things,' she said evasively.

'And the boy? Jackie do you *really* feel he cares about you? Or is it an act? Can't a girl tell? I've always thought a girl would know if a man was genuinely in love with her. That's true, isn't it?'

'I . . . I suppose so.'

She had known that Jonathan was not in love with her, hadn't she?

'Well . . . '

'It's none of your business,' she said, her lips tight. Why did he have to question her like this about someone else?

'Jonathan, why did you come down here in the first place?' she asked. 'You weren't booked in for your own holiday, were you?'

This time it was his turn to look taken aback.

'Why not? Can you think of anywhere more lovely for a holiday? Just as lovely, perhaps . . . but *more* lovely?'

'It won't wash, Jonathan. You just suddenly turned up.'

He sighed and pushed a meringue confection aside. 'All right, Jackie. Your mother was a little worried about you. I . . . I've been going to see her quite a lot. She was on her own, you see.'

'She *likes* being on her own.'

'Perhaps she does, but she likes people nearby her, too. I . . . I felt I wanted to . . . well, keep an eye on her.' He grinned for a moment. 'As a matter of fact, I think she rumbled me and felt I was being a bit of a watchdog and she became a little bit cross. Though I soon realised that her impatience stemmed from a feeling of uneasiness . . . over you! You write to her whenever you can, don't you, my dear? You write quickly, great scrawls, long rambling letters. I've had one or two, and I know.'

She flushed, but said nothing.

'And it's easy to read between the lines. Janet picked out all the points I've just outlined, and she had more or less decided to come and see for herself what was going on. Only I volunteered to come instead.'

'And she agreed?'

'It was better. I booked in here at this hotel. I could observe better looking out on it all. Those people think I'm just here to enjoy myself, not to keep an eye on them. I've just talked to them in a casual friendly way.'

And looked like a representative of the Law, thought Jackie, then bit her lip, her heart suddenly leaping. If she told Jonathan that, it would have all sorts of sinister meanings for him, and now, sitting here in this pleasant dining-room with the warm sunshine beating on her, the whole thing seemed ridiculous.

'They'll all be going on Saturday,' she said.

'Maybe it's all nonsense, built up in the first place out of jealousy.'

'Jealousy?' Surely he couldn't be jealous!

'Yes. Aunt Hetty being jealous of Naismith's attentions to her sister.'

'Oh.' She felt deflated.

'But we'll see, Jackie. As you say, they'll be going soon, then we can forget all about it. Look, my dear, let's forget all about it for the time being. It's a lovely day and I would love a ride on one of those open-top buses, along to Babbacombe, perhaps. When you've finished that coffee, we'll walk along to the bus stop. Let's just forget all about it. Pretend I've only just come.'

She looked at him, and found herself responding to his mood. It *was* a lovely day, and she would enjoy a bus ride. She loved looking at the beautiful gardens and palm trees, the sea calm and soothing as it washed gently against the shore. It would be nice to forget all about the Naismiths and, just for a little while, have Jonathan belong to her.

'All right,' she agreed. 'Let's go.'

Together they walked hand in hand along with the milling crowds of holidaymakers, and the day became one of enchantment for Jackie. At Babbacombe they had tea in a Swedish restaurant and walked through a model village, the miniature landscaping a delight to both of them.

Going home in the evening, Jonathan's hand was warm on her own.

'Jackie!' he said urgently, 'when you turned me down, was it . . . was it because you really felt we were being pushed into it? Was it because of the parents, or . . . or did you feel like that, too?'

It was a lovely evening, the scent of flowers intoxicating and the coloured lights giving the place an almost fairy-tale beauty. Jackie felt almost drugged, wanting to tell him that it was because she had thought he didn't love her. If only he would ask her again . . .

But fairy tales don't last, she reminded herself. It would all be switched off again when the pretty lights went out, then Jonathan would feel trapped, and her heart would be torn with brief happiness snatched away.

'I'm tired, Jonathan,' she said, her voice growing matter-of-fact. 'We'll discuss anything more tomorrow. Ask me then.'

'I'll drive you home.'

'I've got my car, remember? You were waiting for a telephone call . . . '

'I'll drive it home for you.'

'Don't be silly.'

'I'll walk back. I'll need that walk.'

'All right,' she agreed.

It wasn't midnight, but it should have been. The coach had turned into a pumpkin.

'I should like to ring you tomorrow,' said Jonathan. 'I'm still not satisfied,

Jackie. There's a lot which needs to be explained.'

'All right,' she agreed. 'Come along to the house, if you like.'

'As a matter of fact, I may have a friend with me, but I can tell you when I ring. That telephone call I mentioned. Goodnight, Jackie, take care.'

With a swift movement he kissed her soundly, then strode back towards Paignton, leaving Jackie to wonder about the friend. It couldn't be Janetta . . . could it? He couldn't do such a thing to her . . .

She felt the bitterness of jealousy again, as she let herself into the house. Jonathan was such a puzzle to her, he more than anyone. He could treat her casually, then be thoughtful for her. He had vague uneasy feelings that all was not well, yet he could be insensitive enough to bring a friend along when he wanted to see her again. Ten to one it would be Janetta Hodge!

The light was on in the sitting-room, and Jackie paused, surprised. The aunts always went to bed early. Had they a visitor? she wondered. Surely *not* Derek Naismith!

But when she pushed open the door they were alone, looking rather white and subdued.

'Aunt Maude! Hetty! You're late up. Is everything all right?'

'Oh, we're so glad you're back, Jackie darling,' said Hetty, jumping up. 'Isn't the young man with you? Has he gone?'

'Yes. I thought it was too late to ask him in, and that we might disturb you . . .'

'Someone else has disturbed us,' said Maude, 'while we were all out this evening. Hetty and I went to the Flower Club. Nothing's been taken, dear, but my best flower pot is broken where it's been knocked over, and a window has also been broken.'

'Have you sent for the police?' asked Jackie.

'No, dear. We . . . we didn't think we wanted to do that, just yet.'

'Why not?'

'Well, the police . . . it's such bad publicity. These things get around.'

'You aren't running the boarding house now,' said Jackie. 'You don't have to worry about publicity here, and the police aren't likely to rush off and tell people. In any case, how can you be blamed for a break-in?'

'We should take more precautions,' said Maude firmly. 'The police would be right to be cross with us. I mean, we didn't leave a light on, as we normally do, to *pretend* we're still at home, and the radio on to make people think we're listening to music or something.'

'I think we should tell the police.'

'Well, it's too late now,' said Aunt Maude, suddenly firm, 'and we're all tired. As I say, nothing was taken. Maybe we surprised the thief when we came back home. Hetty *thought* she heard a thump. Perhaps he was getting away.'

'I've put hardboard in the window,' said Hetty, rather proudly. 'We'll lock up carefully, though, and get a burglar alarm fitted tomorrow. That should be all right for the police, shouldn't it?'

'Yes,' said Jackie.

Suddenly she was fiercely glad that Jonathan was not too far away. Was this one more pointer to the Naismiths? Was there something in the house they wanted?

Yet what could it be? The odds and ends were all owned by the aunts. There were no precious pictures, or specially good silver. And anyway, what they had was still untouched. Tomorrow she would spend the morning searching the place from top to bottom, on the pretence that she was helping the aunts with housework. That way she could examine everything and see if it gave her any clue to the break-in.

But in spite of her weariness, it was a long time before she slept, then it was a haunting sleep full of uneasy dreams.

8

Next morning she was far from being at her best, as she came downstairs to another morning of sunshine.

Aunt Maude was busily re-potting her geranium which had been knocked off the window ledge the previous evening.

'It couldn't have been a cat, could it?' asked Jackie.

'Oh, my dear . . . have you seen the window?' asked Maude. 'It would have to be a tiger leaping straight for it. No, it was a person . . . a small person, I would think. If you ask me, there's a hooligan element around, with lots of the wrong type of young people. No doubt one of them ran short of money, and decided to break in. But Hetty and I just don't keep money in the house, as you know. They wouldn't find a penny.'

'But they could have stolen something to sell.'

'Oh no, dear. That way they'd get caught. No, if there was no money, they would probably try somewhere else. Well, it's only cost us a window. I'm arranging to have it replaced this morning.'

Hetty was on the telephone while Jackie ate a rather late breakfast. She'd had little left to do to the portrait, and had decided to finish it first of all. Then she felt a freedom taking hold of her such as she hadn't experienced before. Adrian could have the picture as soon as he called for it. She would say goodbye to the Naismiths, and she felt she never wanted to see any of them again. They had a depressing effect on her, especially when she had guilty feelings about feeling this way. There was no denying that Adrian was a very handsome young man, she thought, looking at his portrait. But it almost seemed as though by painting him, she had used up all her admiration for him, and now it was a portait she preferred to forget.

'Hello, dear,' said Hetty, coming in from the telephone. 'That was your young man . . . '

'I don't *have* a young man, Aunt Hetty!'

'Jonathan, of course. I rather think he considers himself your young man. Anyway, he's coming here for lunch today. I've invited him.'

'Oh,' said Jackie, then again she felt her spirits lifting. Maybe things were gradually getting better after all. She remembered again the quick kiss Jonathan had given her last night. He needn't have kissed her, if he didn't want to. Perhaps that meant something after all.

'Good. I'll set the dining table. Our best silver and glass. Four places.'

'No, five. He's bringing a friend.'

Jackie's heart went cold again.

'Did he say who?'

'No . . . no . . . He didn't really say anything about his friend, and I don't really know if it's a man or a woman.'

Jackie thought she knew, and wondered moodily, if there was any way of getting out of the lunch. It would be a bit rich if she had to sit through a meal staring at Jonathan with Janetta Hodge. No doubt that lady would be coming down for a couple of days, probably with business papers for Jonathan.

But why bring her here? Jackie could find no answer to that, and thought that her own jealousy was carrying her into ridiculous notions. She would help the aunts to clean up . . . she had already decided to do that the previous evening . . . then she would put on her best dress, which was black with sleeves like candy-striped balls, and be prepared for whoever came with Jonathan.

Aunt Maude opened the door to both of them at twelve-thirty, and Jackie found herself shaking hands with a powerfully-built young man with springy brown hair and keen grey eyes.

'This is Tom Dennison. We knew each other at school, and he's decided to have a few days in Paignton. I . . . I thought it would be nice if he met all of you.'

Jonathan looked awkward, and Jackie shook Tom's hand politely. Just what was behind this visit? she wondered.

But already the aunts were welcoming the young men, delighted to be entertaining guests to lunch again.

'Are you from London, Mr Dennison?' asked Hetty, as she served out one of her delicious soups.

'No. I'm from the North, Miss Arnold, though I enjoy coming to London. I admit that I'm entranced with Devon, too. Just look at the view out of that window, for instance. Was anything ever more delightful?'

'Yes, it does give us a lot of pleasure,' Hetty admitted, pleased.

'Have you always lived here?' asked Tom Dennison.

'Oh no. Not in *this* house, but we kept a boarding house for a great many years, Maude and I.'

'I bet you met all sorts of people. It

must have given you quite an insight into the human character. You'll get well used to weighing people up . . . a rather frightening ability to people just meeting you for the first time.'

Tom Dennison's eyes were twinkling, but there was a serious note to his questions.

'One would think so,' Maude agreed, 'but it's only so to a certain extent. You see, people on holiday aren't always the same as they are at home. Some turn slightly aggressive because they're paying for service, and expect to get it. Others turn shy and quiet, away from their own background. We've seen people changing on the day they leave, from the day they came. In between they've been out a great deal of the time. It doesn't always make for lasting friendships, except with people who like to come back year after year.'

'Did you get many like that?'

'One or two. Others like to see more places, and choose somewhere different every year.'

'I'm afraid I hop about,' said Jonathan, 'but I think one does if one's interested in architecture. I like to see what sort of buildings go to make a town, and to find out a little about their history. Sometimes one can learn by other people's mistakes.'

'Yes, and nowhere do mistakes show up more clearly than in architecture,' laughed Tom.

'Or painting, perhaps,' put in Jonathan, his eyes full of mischief as he turned to Jackie. 'We have a very talented young artist right here.'

'You must show me some of your work,' said Tom. 'I'm very interested.'

'I . . . I don't have many pictures here,' Jackie excused herself. 'Just a few seascapes . . .'

'And a portrait, dear,' said Maude. 'Don't forget that portrait of Adrian Naismith. Why, she finished it only this morning.'

Jackie could sense the quickened interest in Tom Dennison. Who was he, she wondered, and why had Jonathan brought him? If she and Jon had been engaged, she could well understand it. He might easily have his eye on Tom as a good best man! But there was no question of an engagement between them.

Yet this young man was more than usually interested in her pictures. Could he be an expert of some kind that Jon had remembered? He had never mentioned this young man to her before, nor could she remember him in the old days when boys used to come and stay at the Lodge.

'Are you professionally interested in art?' she asked, turning to the newcomer.

'Er . . . no. Not exactly. But I love looking at pictures, and I have been known to buy one now and again if it took my fancy. I doubt if I'd ever commission you to paint my portrait, Miss . . . er . . . Jackie. I avoid a looking glass as far as possible.'

'Oh, it isn't that bad!' she said, laughing.

Whatever he was, she felt instinctively that she liked him and could trust him.

'We'll have coffee in the lounge,' said Hetty. 'Then this time Maude and I will clear away, and you show Mr Dennison your paintings, dear. You do have some interesting ones, you know.'

'Excellent idea, except that I feel Jonathan and I ought to be doing some of the chores . . . '

'And you a guest! Never!' said Hetty. 'Besides, we value our crystal and won't even let Jackie lay a finger on it.'

They all laughed, and Jackie led the way into the lounge where large settees and chairs were grouped round the coffee table, beside the fine bay window with the magnificent view of Goodrington North Sands.

After coffee, Jackie brought her seascapes, and felt Tom Dennison's genuine interest, especially in a small oil sketch which she had set aside for framing after it was ready to be varnished.

'This is one I would like to buy,' he

told her, after long and careful study.

She felt rather embarrassed, wondering if Jonathan had bulldozed him into it.

'Oh . . . perhaps you ought to think about it . . . it isn't quite ready for framing yet. They have to harden over a long period.'

'No, I don't want time to think about it. I wouldn't sleep till I had it. I'm like that with pictures, if I can afford them at all. If I fall in love with one, I keep thinking about it till it's mine. This is going to be one of my favourites.'

'I *knew* it was your thing, Tom,' said Jonathan, laughing. 'I almost put a bet on that you wouldn't be able to resist it.' Then his eyes grew serious. 'Bring the portrait now, Jackie. Please, dear.'

She went to obey, feeling that the atmosphere had suddenly changed, and returned carrying Adrian's picture.

Tom Dennison rose to his full height, looking older as he went to examine the picture.

'Well?' asked Jonathan.

'I don't know. You must understand we've never had any dealings with him, or his father, though there has been a girl of the description. Not Naismith, though.'

'You know nothing about them, then?'

'I'm going into it. We had much that was unexplained . . . '

'Look, what is all this?' asked Jackie. 'Why are you so interested in Adrian's portrait?'

Both young men looked at her gravely.

'Tom's a police officer,' said Jonathan quietly. 'As I say, I didn't like the sound of the Naismiths and the way they were worming themselves in here. I suspected it was for a purpose, so I wondered if they'd been doing anything at home which was suspicious. I rang up Tom.'

'I was due a holiday anyway,' Tom smiled, 'and I might as well spend it with old Jonathan in this lovely place. I just thought I would run an eye over things, much as two ladies would run an eye over prospective guests. So far these people don't seem to have done anything wrong. You've missed nothing from the house?'

'N . . . no.'

'What does that mean?'

'There was a break-in last night.'

'What?' cried Jonathan. 'When?'

'While we were all out. The only casualties were the window and a geranium in a pot. Nothing was taken.'

'Have they even *hinted* at being interested in anything in this house?' asked Tom, after he had asked Jackie to tell him its complete history. 'Nothing in drawers or cupboards since the old days? Nothing left behind?'

'Nothing,' said Jackie. 'The aunts are very thorough, and everything had to be immaculate before they put it to their own use.'

'Of course. I know what you mean. May I see round?'

Jackie took him over the house, pausing to tell the aunts, who were pleased by his interest. Blushing a little, she took them into her own rather untidy bedroom. She had rather left it in order to finish the picture, then there had been so little time to tidy up after she had helped the aunts to prepare for Jon and his friend coming for lunch.

Now several items of clothing lay on the bed, and her dressing table had a thin film of spilled powder. In a corner she had stacked more stretched canvases and boxes of paints and brushes. An easel lurched drunkenly against the attic door.

'Oh dear,' she said, scarlet-faced. 'I didn't think I'd be showing anyone round. I . . . I'd intended to do this room out properly this afternoon.'

Jonathan's face registered mock disapproval.

'Obviously it's all your own stuff,' laughed Tom, thinking of the other two spartan bedrooms. 'Was it, too, completely empty when you came?'

'Completely.'

'Have you entertained the Naismith girl . . . is it Cynthia? . . . in here? Has she had the freedom of your upstairs apartments?'

'I don't think so,' said Jackie, leading the way back down to the lounge. 'There's a downstairs cloakroom. Cynthia and I were never close friends. She isn't an awfully happy girl.'

'No? I wonder why,' said Tom. 'Was that your impression, too, Jon?'

'Wary, I'd say,' Jonathan put in. 'She's always on guard, and my charms were wasted on her.'

He grinned again at Jackie, who refused to grin back.

'I think she was . . . was maybe married and separated from her husband,' said Jackie. 'She was secretive about it.'

'Then what gave you that idea?'

'An envelope which fell out of her bag addressed to Cynthia Clarke . . . '

'Clarke!' cried Tom, turning to stare at her. 'Cynthia Clarke. Now that does interest me.'

'Why?' asked Jonathan. 'What's she done?'

But Tom was pursing his lips, lost in thought.

'I'll have to go into it,' he told them. 'You say that they're all going home soon?'

'Day after tomorrow. Adrian is coming up for his picture. They've been seeing the sights this past couple of days or so . . . last fling before they leave.'

'Then just give him his picture and say goodbye. I shouldn't keep up any friendship with these people, Jackie. They're probably all right, but sometimes people have activities which are on the fringe of the law. I'm not saying the Naismiths are criminals, my dear, but they might not have the integrity you're used to.'

Jackie found this a trifle vague for her, and looked back at him doubtfully.

'Maybe Jackie won't find that so easy,' said Jonathan rather harshly, his eyes on her face, then flickering to the portrait. She flushed angrily and bit back a reply.

The aunts came bustling in, and Jackie wondered if she ought to say anything, then decided against it. One more day and they would all be gone. Why worry them needlessly?

'I've had a lovely morning,' said Tom Dennison, 'and I've got myself a picture I'll treasure for a long time to come.'

'Which one?' asked Hetty eagerly. 'I like that one. I enjoyed watching Jackie work on it.'

'Oh, Aunt Hetty! Perhaps I should have given it to you.'

'And missed a sale! You would have been offering it to me as a gift probably, but now you've sold it to Mr Dennison.'

'And very pleased he is with it,' said Tom. 'Goodbye, Miss Arnold . . . Miss Hetty . . . Jackie.'

'Do come again,' said Aunt Maude. 'We so enjoyed your company.'

'I shan't promise, but I will if I can.'

'I'll ring you,' said Jonathan, his hand

grasping Jackie's arm. His eyes were speculative as he looked at her.

She nodded and they walked down the path to Jonathan's car, waving cheerfully.

'What a nice young man,' said Hetty. 'So he's fond of art . . . he must be an architect like Jonathan. We forgot to ask him, didn't we?'

Jackie said nothing. Now she was looking forward to getting rid of the portrait to Adrian, and saying goodbye to him. After that . . . after that her heart would probably take wings with relief.

⋆　⋆　⋆

Jackie had to go shopping the following afternoon, and she hesitated a little before leaving the house. There had been no word from the Naismiths, and she felt she only wanted to talk to them long enough to hand over the portrait.

'If they call in while I'm out, then I shan't be long,' she told Maude. 'If

Adrian wants to take it before I get back, then please tell him it must be kept flat till it dries, and remember, about six months before varnishing.'

'All right, dear, I'll tell him. Are you likely to be long?'

Jackie grinned. 'I have Tom Dennison's cheque to pay into the bank. That should make my account a little healthier, and I want to buy some toilet things. Can I get you or Aunt Hetty anything?'

She made a list, and the two older ladies watched her go. The man had now finished putting in the window and Hetty was clearing away the mess, and gently rubbing any putty marks.

'You're not supposed to do all that till it hardens,' said Maude severely.

'I'm being gentle. Hardly touching it.'

'Well . . .'

'Oh, Maude, stop fussing!'

They were still inclined to snap at one another, thought Maude as she turned away. A short while later she looked out of the window and saw all three Naismiths coming in the gate.

'Here they all are, Hetty,' she called. 'Come to say goodbye. Shall we offer them sherry instead of coffee?'

'There isn't enough,' said Hetty sharply, then relented. 'Sorry, my dear. Yes, we'll have sherry by all means, and a nice piece of my special fruit cake. After all, it's their last day.'

Perhaps because of this, Hetty was more cordial than usual to the holiday visitors who had rather gone out of their way to become their friends.

Hetty remembered a cat they had once had which had arrived on their doorsep, as a kitten, and had insisted on staying. Gradually she had become used to it, then she had ended up by loving it very much. She doubted, however, that she would ever feel the same way about the Naismiths!

'Ah, well Hetty, this is rather a sad visit,' Derek was saying heartily, 'when we must say cheerio. For now, that is. There's always another year.'

'Heaven forbid!' thought Hetty, and turned to Cynthia.

'All packed, then?'

'Not yet. We go after breakfast in the morning.'

'You've been buying new things, though. You'll have to get your brother to sit on your case for you.'

Maude was talking to Adrian, inviting him to sit on an easy chair by the coffee table.

'Er . . . ' She looked over at Hetty.

'We'll have sherry today,' said Hetty, 'since it *is* your last visit. Sit down and I'll just get the decanter and glasses.'

'Oh no, please. We have a better idea,' said Derek, looking expansive. 'We've actually come to invite you all out. Our treat!'

'Oh, but I'm afraid Jackie is still out shopping,' Hetty protested.

She did not particularly want to go out, for whatever sort of treat. It would mean putting on her best suit which was becoming uncomfortably tight.

'She has finished the picture, but you

mustn't touch it yet. It must be kept flat when you take it home. That was the message in case you called and had to leave again before she got back. And she sent her best wishes for a safe journey home.'

'She couldn't have thought I would leave without seeing her,' said Adrian.

'Well . . . perhaps she thought you would write . . .'

'I owe her money, not the other way round, which *could* account for her sneaking off out of my way.' He sounded sarcastic.

'Oh, I don't think she's doing that!'

'I should hope not!' said Derek, 'after the happy times we've all had together this past three weeks or so. That's why I insist you are all my guests today. That's what we want, isn't it, Cynthia?'

'Oh, sure,' she said. 'A real party.'

She hardly looked in the mood to enjoy herself, thought Hetty.

'Well, we may as well all be comfortable,' she said. 'Or at least, you can wait till Maude and I change. By that time Jackie might be home.'

'You only need a coat and hat,' Derek insisted firmly. 'We don't want to make a stiff formal occasion of it. I tell you what, I'll walk with you ladies down to the restaurant we've chosen, and Adrian can wait for Jackie. They'll want to discuss the fee for the picture, anyhow.'

Hetty thought she had got the message. A fee for the picture! It made sense that Adrian wanted to discuss it with Jackie on her own. Perhaps he hoped she would give it to him . . .

Hetty pulled up her uncharitable thoughts. No, the Naismiths were not mean, whatever they were. In fact, it was Jackie who had suggested the portrait, wasn't it? She *hadn't* wanted to take a fee, but he had insisted on buying the picture. Maybe he wanted to offer her more than they had agreed.

On the other hand, they wouldn't have something more *personal* to discuss, would they? wondered Hetty uneasily. Theirs had been a holiday friendship, and holiday friendships did not last . . . for the most part.

'We'll take our time,' Derek was saying, 'and enjoy the sea air and sunshine. The youngsters will probably beat us to it in the car.'

'Oh, all right,' Hetty agreed. If they were going to be quick, then no doubt she was worrying herself needlessly. And it might be rather nice to go out for a change. 'Shall we put a hat on, Maude?'

Oddly enough it was Maude who was most reluctant to go.

'There's really no need to go to such expense,' she protested. 'Surely a nice glass of sherry . . . '

'*Your* sherry, my dear. *Your* hospitality again. No, this time it must come from us. You must all be *our* guests. Maybe Jackie will be back by the time you're ready, and we won't have our nice leisurely walk.'

The older ladies hesitated no longer, but hurried upstairs to run a comb through greying curls, and put on straw hats which were frilly contrasts to their good plain coats.

'Would you care for something while you're waiting?' Hetty asked Adrian.

He pulled a paperback from his pocket, and sat down in his comfortable chair again.

'No, thanks. This is fine. I enjoy a few pages at odd moments.'

'It's my favourite pursuit!' said Maude. 'Reading. I do enjoy Jane Austen, though I find some modern books quite entertaining. What are you reading, Adrian?'

'Now, we mustn't get started on the subject of books,' interrupted Derek, hastily. 'Come on, Maude. How nice you look in that hat!'

Maude failed to look pleased by the compliment. She glanced at Hetty, then at Adrian sitting quietly by the window.

'Wouldn't it be better if we all waited, then we could all go together?' she suggested. 'Jackie shouldn't be long now.'

'We can't *all* squeeze into the car,' said Derek. 'No, Maude, this is best.

Believe me, Adrian won't lose Jackie in broad daylight. She knows the place a lot better than he does, anyway.'

'Of course not,' agreed Maude, and relaxed a little. 'We'll go, then,' she agreed, drawing on her navy gloves.

'Lead the way, Cynthia,' boomed Derek. 'The restaurant is expecting us. I booked this morning.'

Hetty followed Cynthia, and Derek took Maude's arm, though she glanced back now and again till they were out of sight. She just did not like leaving someone alone in their house, though short of being downright rude, she did not know what she could do about it. After all, she had nothing to go on but her own feelings.

Until the house was out of sight, she could still see the faint outline of Adrian sitting in the large chair by the window.

9

Jackie used her key, then pushed open the front door, dumping some of her packages in the hall. She carried Aunt Hetty's basket into the kitchen. It was deserted, and she paused, uncertainly, a faint aroma of cigarette smoke in the air.

'Aunt Hetty!' she called. 'Maude!'

She heard a faint sound and hurried through to the sitting-room where the cigarette smoke was stronger, her eyes going to a used ashtray.

So Cynthia had been here, at least! There was lipstick on the cigarette ends, and neither the aunts nor herself smoked. Cynthia and Adrian? Derek? Perhaps the picture had gone, she thought hopefully. But if so, where were the aunts?

Again she heard the faint dull thud from above, and ran out into the hall.

Maybe one of them was upstairs in the bedrooms.

Jackie took the stairs two at a time, but saw that Aunt Maude and Aunt Hetty had left their bedroom doors wide open, and that the faint movement came from her own bedroom.

'Aunt Maude?' she said, pushing open the door.

Then her heart leapt to her mouth, then hammered loudly enough for her to hear it, as Adrian grinned at her from the bed where he was stretched out, hands behind his head, contemplating his own portrait which was still on the easel.

'Hello, darling,' he said. 'I've been waiting for you. You did a pretty nice job on me, and that gives me lots of encouragement.'

'What are you doing here? On my bed, too. Get off!'

'Steady on,' he drawled. 'Don't go flying into a paddy.'

'Well, I don't like people just calmly walking into my bedroom . . .'

'Wanted to see my portrait, of course.'

'Well, I'd have brought it down. Where are the aunts?'

'All out celebrating, darling, with Father and Cyn. Celebrating getting rid of the obnoxious Naismiths who've been a thorn in their lily-white flesh for the past week or two. Yours, too.'

Jackie didn't bother to deny it.

'Why *did* you keep coming?' she asked curiously.

'Don't be so modest. Can't you believe it was for your beauty and charm?'

'No.'

She was rather tired, and felt that only the truth would suffice.

'No. You've gone all out to be nice to all of us. Your father cultivated Maude, since Hetty would have none of him, and even your sister has made herself be nice to me, though I don't believe she likes me in the least.'

She was crossing over to take the picture off the easel, but he reached out and pulled her dress, then grabbed her to him, holding her closely.

'*They're* not *me*, my sweet. I know why I came. Come on, don't be so rigid. Loosen up a bit.'

She was holding herself like a ramrod in his arms, her heart beating wildly with anger, and a touch of fear which he seemed to sense immediately.

'Not afraid of me, are you, love?' he asked, very softly.

'I'm angry,' she said. 'I don't *want* you in my bedroom. Please go!'

'Don't be prissy. You're the wrong generation. Come on, love.'

He began to kiss her and she struggled wildly, fighting him off as he laughed and grabbed for her again. She heard a faint sound downstairs, but she was too busy being furious and rather terrified of Adrian to notice. He really did look wolfish, she thought.

'This is why I love you, darling,' he was saying. 'At least you've got spirit and you're much more fun, though you should curb your temper at times.'

He grabbed her again and was kissing her fiercely when the bedroom door was pushed open and Jonathan looked in.

'I thought I heard . . . Jackie!'

She struggled free. 'Jon . . . '

'Oh, darling,' said Adrian, laughing, 'didn't you lock the door?'

'Jonathan, I . . . '

'What are you doing here?' he asked, his face hard and white as he looked at Adrian.

'I was invited, of course. You don't think I'd calmly walk up here all by myself, do you? Or if I did, and Jackie objected . . . '

'No!' she cried. 'Jon . . . '

He stared at her, his dark eyes sparking with fire.

'I don't expect you need me,' he told her, looking at her dishevelled hair. 'Sorry to have interrupted.'

She said nothing. She had appealed to him, and he had chosen to believe Adrian Naismith, who was laughing almost helplessly, as Jonathan ran back downstairs.

'He hasn't even waited to shut the door,' he said. 'What an exit!'

'Go!' she said, the anger now making her calm and determined. 'You can take your portrait if you want it, but I want no payment. Just get out. You can shut the door after *you*.'

'Not without one little thing, darling.'

She turned white.

'Don't you want to know what it is?'

'No! There's nothing here for you.'

'Oh, but that's where you're wrong, love. I want the key to the attic.'

His voice had gone very soft, and now suddenly it was harder and he grabbed her arm.

'Stop it! You're hurting me!'

'I'll hurt you a lot more, darling, if you don't produce it. I know you have it. It's always been kept in the door, you see, and it isn't anywhere in this room . . . '

'How do you know?'

'It's been searched, of course.'

'By you? The other night, while we were out?'

'I couldn't have got through such a small pane, darling, and I can't search as thoroughly as Cynthia.'

'So it was Cynthia!'

'Why not? She's as agile as a monkey.'

'But . . . ' She was bewildered. He had hold of her wrist and she was suddenly aware of the strength of his fingers and fear shot through her again. 'Why do you want it? It's empty, but for a few boxes. They're empty, too.'

'I know what's in there, and I know that the only means of getting up there is through that door. The skylight is too small, even for . . . '

'Cynthia?'

'Yes, darling. Cynthia. As I say, she's as agile as a monkey.'

She remembered the odd thumping noises which had frightened her so much one night, and the vague menace which they had all felt about the place.

'Why do you want to go into the

attic?' she repeated.

'That's my business. Come on now, where's the key? Where have you put it?'

Jackie had barely noticed the key which she had hung round her neck for safe keeping. After a while it had become part of her like a piece of jewellery constantly worn. But now the small key seemed to grow until it became a lump of metal round her neck, and was pressing hard against her chest.

'I didn't think it was important,' she said, as casually as she could. 'It's lost. We never use the attic.'

'Don't talk rubbish, or tell lies. It's naughty to tell lies.'

'I'm going!' she cried, and ran for the door, but Adrian was there before her, his fluid movements suddenly menacing.

'No, you don't, love. I really want that key.'

'If you tell me *why* you want it, then maybe we can look for it.'

Her brain seemed to be working at fever pitch. Her aunts had gone out with Derek and Cynthia Naismith. How long would it be before they came back? How long? Thank goodness Jonathan had at least left the door open . . .

A hard lump was rising in her throat when she thought of Jonathan. She had loved and wanted him so much, but when she needed him desperately, he had walked out, thinking the worst. How could he? she thought, her body shuddering with fright and revulsion. How could he think such a thing! If only Tom Dennison had come with him . . .

Tom Dennison! Could she somehow get in touch with Tom? Even as her thoughts whirled, she heard the door opening and the sound of footsteps downstairs.

'They're back! Thank God they're back!'

The relief was so enormous that she almost collapsed on to the floor, wanting to laugh till she cried. Adrian looked like a cat ready to spring.

Then the footsteps stopped.

'Adrian! Are you there?'

He relaxed visibly, and Jackie felt physically sick when she heard Cynthia's voice at the foot of the stairs.

'Up here, darling,' he called. 'In the bedroom.'

It was a different girl who appeared round the door, as though her body had been strengthened by a rod of steel. The rather insipid face was now purposeful, her eyes hard and bright.

'What kept you?' she asked. 'The two old dears won't wait any longer. They're on their way home. I said I'd got to telephone, and ran on ahead. Your father is making them dawdle, though, since it's a nice day. He's an expert on the job.'

'I can't find the damn key! I've looked everywhere.'

'We should never have left it to the last minute like this, or one of us should have stayed on. Have you looked in her bag?'

'What do you think?'

Jackie was looking from one to the other, stupefied.

She felt she was living in a nightmare. These people were criminals, she thought disbelievingly. Nobody would behave as they were doing unless they were afraid of the law. As it was they were breaking the law by breaking into the house and holding her like this. Or could they claim that they had been invited into the house?

She stared at Cynthia, taking in the difference in the girl, and remembered that Tom Dennison had been struck by her name, and had told her they might be on the fringes of the law.

'You said '*your* father' to Adrian,' she remembered suddenly. 'What do you mean, *your* father? Isn't he yours, too?'

Cynthia grinned, coming over to look at her and examining her suit for pockets. She had already rummaged through items of clothing, making Jackie's lip curl. She hated seeing her things being pawed over by this girl.

'Oh yes, Jackie dear, he's my father. In law, that is.'

'In law? You're adopted?'

'*Father*-in-law, love. Surely you've heard of a father-in-law?'

Jackie took a minute to work this out.

'You're married to . . . but your name is Clarke, surely . . . Cynthia Clarke.'

'I *knew* she was on to it! She's sharper than she looks.'

Cynthia glanced again at Adrian, who was again sitting down on the bed. How long would the aunts be?

'Mrs Clarke? I knew you were married, but . . . '

'Not nearly so sharp after all,' laughed Cynthia. 'Any fool would have twigged that Adrian's my husband long before now.'

The news came to Jackie almost like a release, as though a picture in her mind had been distorted, and now it clicked into place.

'Of course!' she said. 'That's it. I should have realised.'

'Then where's that key?' asked Cynthia. 'It can only be *on* you. We've looked everywhere else.'

'One place you haven't looked,' said Jackie, confidence beginning to soar. She was no longer afraid of these people, and her contempt showed in her eyes. 'It didn't occur to you that we would give the key to someone else.'

'Your friend Jonathan? I admit he scared me at first. I thought he was a policeman . . . he *looks* like the law, but we know now that he's a harmless type after all. He draws little houses.'

'He's just been, darling,' drawled Adrian. 'Got frightened by naughty behaviour!'

'He's probably gone for a friend of his,' said Jackie calmly. 'He isn't stupid either. The friend who kept the attic key.'

This time Jackie felt she had them guessing.

'Who?'

'Tom Dennison. *He* really is a policeman.'

Cynthia went grey.

'I knew it!' she cried, rounding on Adrian. 'I knew there was something wrong. For heaven's sake, leave it. Come on!'

She rushed for the top of the stairs, and after a furious look, Adrian was after her.

'Don't panic, Cyn!' he cried. 'How do we know . . . '

'Don't argue,' she called back. 'Just come on!'

Jackie's knees shook as she heard the door slamming, then she sat with her head between her knees as sickness swept over her. It seemed hours before the two aunts walked in, and Jackie walked shakily down the stairs, then burst into tears.

'They were so quick, it was really quite rude,' Maude was saying. 'Jackie! Jackie, my dear, where were you? What kept you?'

Alarm was spreading over their faces as the tears came, then they became briskly efficient, giving her something to drink and letting her cry.

'It . . . it wasn't Adrian, was it?' asked Hetty. Jackie managed to smile, feeling their quick anxiety.

'Not in the way you mean. But they're crooks of some sort, darlings. There's something hidden in the attic. They must have left it here when they used to rent the house, only when they came back to collect, they found that it was now sold.'

'Oh.'

Understanding began to dawn as Jackie began to tell the whole story.

'No wonder the Naismith man seemed shattered, though he pretended it was because of his wife. Perhaps it was.'

'His wife might still be alive. They've told so many lies,' said Jackie wearily. 'Cynthia is Adrian's wife.'

'His wife!'

The aunts looked at one another, then at Jackie, feeling suddenly frightened. They'd had a brush with things far removed from their normal life, and it all felt strange and unreal.

'I . . . I'm going to ring Jonathan,' said Maude tremulously.

'No!'

Jackie startled all of them by the strength of her denial. The aunts stared at her. 'No,' she said, more quietly, 'Jonathan can't help. We need Tom Dennison. He's a policeman. He gave me a number to ring if I wanted him. I . . . I think he's been wondering about . . . about the Naismiths. Under suspicion, isn't that it?'

She smiled briefly, and rose.

'I feel better now. I'll ring Tom and give him the attic key.' She drew it out from the chain round her neck. 'I put it there for safe keeping because I'm always losing things, and I felt unsafe with that attic door in my bedroom . . .'

'Oh, my dear!'

'Well, you weren't to know, were you? But if Jonathan calls, I can't see him. I . . . I have something to do.'

'What, dear?' asked Hetty anxiously.

'I want to destroy a picture. I've thrown out practice work many times, and pictures which I felt weren't good enough. But this is the first time I've destroyed a finished work which was perfectly all right.

'And what's more, it's going to give me pleasure to do it.'

*　★　★*

Tom Dennison came down the stairs rather slowly and wearily, an untidy parcel in his hands, which were filthy with soot.

'You haven't had a fire all summer, I presume?' he asked the aunts.

'No. It's much too warm. We use the electric in the evenings if we feel chilly.'

'That's what I thought, though you probably would not have noticed anyway. There's an access flue to the chimney in the attic, and this had been put on a ledge.'

'What is it?' asked Jackie, her eyes wide with fascination.

247

'Printing plates. Illegal fivers. I thought it would be that. Your friend Adrian is a very talented printer, I should think, though no doubt his holiday is due for an extension.'

Jackie looked with curiosity at the plates which Tom had carefully uncovered, and just as carefully wrapped up again in the soiled cloth before using the clean brown paper Aunt Maude had produced.

'There's probably fingerprints,' he said, 'since they were so keen to get them back.'

It seemed years since she had rung Tom Dennison, and had to wait for his return to the hotel before he contacted her.

'I . . . I think you ought to come round,' she said, and he had answered crisply that he would be right with her.

'He's coming,' she said to the aunts, after putting down the phone. She knew they were looking at her curiously, wondering why she had not wanted to contact Jonathan, but they had too much tact to question her.

Jackie noticed almost the same sort of difference in Tom Dennison that she had noticed in Cynthia, as though a professional cloak had fallen on their shoulders. It was strange what similarity there could be in complete contrast.

'And you say you felt frightened of that attic door, and locked it?'

'Yes. I could never really put my finger on what had frightened me. I kept telling myself it was only mice, or even birds on the roof. Owls, perhaps. But I felt safer with it locked.'

'Oh dear, if only we'd known!' cried Hetty.

'It was only a momentary thing,' said Jackie. 'As soon as I'd locked it, the door became part of the wall. Only I was so afraid I would lose the key . . . you know how easily I lose things . . . At first I just hung it round my neck till I could think of what to do with it, then somehow it just became a habit.'

'And the Naismiths didn't really think of a young girl doing such a thing.

A key like the attic one is hardly an attractive piece of jewellery.'

'No,' said Jackie, then she could not help smiling a little.

'Right,' said Tom. 'This may take some time. I don't suppose that whatever is hidden there will be out on display.'

'There's nothing,' said Aunt Hetty. 'Or it must be very small. We were up several times when we first moved in.'

They made tea and sat about nervously, saying little, while Tom searched the attic using a powerful electric torch, and now the alien property which had caused them all so much fear and unpleasantness was being wrapped up again.

'What now?' asked Jackie.

'Now I'd better have a wash!' grinned Tom. 'We'll try to keep any further unpleasantness to a minimum,' he promised, 'and in the meantime, I could use that cup of tea!'

He saw that the two older ladies needed something to do, and they almost fell on his suggestion with relief, each getting out cups and boiling up the kettle, though it was Jackie who prowled up and down, then sank into a chair feeling more exhausted than she had ever done in her life.

'We'll sell this house again,' said Aunt Maude, after Tom had gone. 'I won't stay here a minute longer than I can help.'

'No, we won't,' Hetty disagreed. 'Those people are not going to turn us out of a house so suitable for our needs. I refuse to let their nastiness make an upheaval for us.'

Tears were welling up in Maude's eyes.

'But it's different for you, Hetty. You were never taken in by them. I was. I . . . I was even flattered for a while when . . . when that man was going all out to make a fool of me. Smarming all over me. Only I . . . I was vain enough to think he meant it. I . . . I feel so ashamed . . . '

'Oh, nonsense, Maude. It just so

happens he picked on you. If he'd picked on me, I'd have done exactly the same. Stop weeping, and blow your nose, then we can start forgetting about it all.'

'I . . . I can't. What a fool I was!'

'If you were a fool, so was I,' said Jackie, coming to sit beside her. 'Don't forget that. I let Adrian take me out. Even . . . even kiss me. So there!'

Aunt Maude's tears began to vanish.

'Oh, Jackie! My dear, you . . . you hadn't fallen in love with him, had you? Is . . . is that why you won't see the other young man?'

Jackie's face froze.

'No, I hadn't fallen in love with him,' she said evenly, 'but I'm only telling you so that you'll recognise you weren't the only foolish one. Doesn't that make you feel better?'

Maude nodded.

'I suppose it does,' she agreed with a rather trembling smile.

Hetty had opened windows and doors to let a gust of fresh air blow through the house.

'There,' she said happily, 'now the house really does feel fresh, and it feels like ours, too, Maude. No one is driving us from our home, and I'm not afraid of the place any more. Which is strange . . . it always seemed to menace us. Now we can really enjoy the rest of the summer with you, Jackie dear.'

'I think I shall want to go home soon, Aunt Hetty,' said Jackie, 'in a day or two, when all this has finally blown over. I think you both really wanted me because you *could* feel the menace, but could not understand it.'

This time it was Hetty's turn to blush.

'Oh well, we wanted you for your own sake, too. We got used to having you down here for a little while at least, during the summer months. We . . . I thought that maybe Maude and I had some adjusting to do, and young company like you would help. I was so afraid the menace came from inside, if you know what I mean.'

She looked at Maude uncertainly.

'Well, it didn't,' her sister declared, and they began to smile. Jackie rose with relief. The household was back to normal.

Maude went to answer the telephone, saying it would probably be that nice Mr Dennison again, but she returned almost immediately.

'For you, Jackie. It . . . it's Jonathan.'

'I don't want to speak to him.'

Maude looked uncertain, then Jackie's chin rose.

'It's all right, Auntie darling. I'll tell him.'

She picked up the receiver.

'I must see you, Jackie.' Jonathan's voice sounded crisp and urgent. 'Please. It's very important.'

'There's nothing you can say to me. I suppose by now you've seen Tom Dennison?'

'Yes, but . . . '

'Then I needn't explain my reasons for refusing to see you, or even wanting to see you again, Jonathan.'

'No . . . don't go, Jackie! I insist that you see me. I'm coming round right now.'

'Don't bother. I'll be in bed. In my bedroom, by myself, and I object to having anyone else invading my privacy. Anyone!'

She hung up, her cheeks flaming with colour and angry tears in her eyes.

But as she climbed the stairs, only the tears were left. Jonathan's voice had still held the power to hurt her. Her anger against him had not killed her love for him.

But she would get over it, she vowed, looking a little bit like her Aunt Hetty. 'I'll get along without him.'

* * *

Jonathan turned up the following morning immediately after breakfast, and after a look at the aunts, Jackie agreed to see him, in the sitting-room. He looked very pale, his face almost grey in spite of the tan he had acquired, but his dark eyes burned fiercely.

'I won't even try to excuse myself,' he told Jackie, as soon as the door closed, 'but I ask you to have a bit of understanding.'

'What about? You took one look and decided that you had the whole situation summed up, even though I appealed to you. I needed help, Jonathan, and you let me down.'

'For goodness' sake, Jackie, have you no imagination? Can't you see how I would feel?'

'I don't care how you felt!' she cried.

The hurt of seeing his eyes condemning her was still there, raw and sore. He said nothing more for a moment, and the words seemed to hang in the air.

'I used to think my stock wasn't very high with the Arnolds,' he said, his mouth twisting a little. 'I don't think even your mother approved of me.'

'She felt you . . . you were inclined to be extravagant and perhaps selfish . . . with your parents . . .'

Her voice faltered a little. 'No, that's

not fair. It was none of our business
. . . your relationship with your parents,
I mean.'

'There we are in agreement,' he said
quietly, 'though it's interesting that
you've seen me as a thoughtless, selfish
type, spending the family cash. No
doubt on wine, women and song.
Janetta, for instance.'

Her cheeks glowed.

'Whatever we thought of one
another, it's all finished. I think we're
quits.'

'Except that I was prepared to
apologise, when temporary loss of
reason clouded my judgement. You're
very quick to condemn, Jackie. Perhaps
. . . perhaps we've hurt one another
enough.'

He was gone, and she sat down on
the chair, and allowed the hot tears to
roll down her cheeks. Aunt Hetty had
slipped in after hearing the door close,
and now she stroked Jackie's hair till
her sobs quietened.

'I'm sorry,' she said, sitting up. 'I

must seem like a fool.'

'Then we're all fools, Jackie. You aren't the first girl to cry over a tiff with her young man.'

'It isn't just a tiff, Aunt Hetty.'

'But you love him, dear.'

'And he doesn't love me. Not really. I . . . I sometimes thought he was beginning to . . . only that didn't last long. He . . . he saw me with Adrian, and just backed out. Even though I told him he was wrong.'

'Perhaps he was hurt and didn't stop to think.'

A tear rolled down her cheek.

'Perhaps he was,' she agreed.

'Then can't you discuss it?'

Slowly Jackie shook her head.

'No. It's all mixed up now. I . . . I rather think I hurt him, too. It's all spoiled now.'

'Maybe it seems so at the moment. Maybe you'll feel better if you leave it for a day or two, and give yourself time to get it all into perspective. This has been a very upsetting time for all of us, and there's much we still don't know. For instance, who put those printing blocks in our attic? I keep wondering about that, if it was Derek Naismith himself. And why here? Why bring them all the way from Liverpool to hide them here?'

'Tom Dennison will tell us,' said Jackie wearily, her head beginning to ache. 'I wonder if Adrian will be arrested. Or Cynthia . . . or will it be Derek Naismith? Perhaps they're a gang.'

'Or members of a gang.'

'You're being dramatic again,' said Maude, coming to join them. 'No doubt Jackie will enjoy telling Janet all about it when she gets home.'

'Enjoy?' cried Jackie.

Maude's glance had flickered at Hetty, and a smile passed between them. They intended to keep the child from brooding.

'Why not? In a way it's all been very exciting.'

'It's the sort of excitement we can

well do without!' said Jackie. 'I'm going home to a quiet life for a little while, then I think I'll go up to London. Maybe I'll go commercial, and try to get a job . . . if I'm good enough.'

'But you'd sell heaps of landscapes and seascapes. And portraits, if you kept on painting them.'

Jackie shuddered. 'Not portraits.'

'When do you plan to go home, dear?' asked Hetty.

'Thursday. I came on a Thursday, so I'll travel back on that day, too. If that's okay with both of you.'

'Janet will be pleased to have you back,' said Maude wistfully.

'Wouldn't you enjoy coming back with me for a few days? The cottage is tiny, but we can all double up for a short time.'

Hetty looked at Maude, then her eyes crinkled.

'No. Thank you very much, Jackie, but I don't think we ought to leave the house empty just now. Someone might break in!'

10

'Printing plates!' cried Janet. 'For goodness' sake, Jackie, how did they get into the house? Into the attic, as well!'

Jackie had arrived home late the previous evening looking completely worn out, and Janet had fussed over her like a mother hen.

'I *knew* it was a mistake to let you go to the aunts,' she said. 'They'd only use you . . . '

'That's nonsense, Mother,' said Jackie sharply. 'They've never 'used' me in their lives. They were glad of my help in the boarding house, but this time I was a guest, and exceedingly well looked after.'

'But you look done up. What kind of holiday can it have been? Did you see Jonathan Nelson, by the way?'

Colour flooded richly into Jackie's

cheeks, and Janet's eyes grew speculative. It was easy to see now why her daughter looked so tired and dispirited. It was Jonathan Nelson!

'Can we talk about it tomorrow, Mother?' Jackie asked, and Janet had lost no time in whisking her off to bed.

Next morning Janet rose early after a rather sleepless night. She was beginning to wonder if Jackie's depressed spirits weren't largely her own doing. After all, she had criticised Jonathan as much as anybody, but now . . .

She pondered deeply as she prepared breakfast, and carried some steaming coffee into Jackie's bedroom.

The girl was still asleep, the hint of tears on her cheeks, and Janet started to back away. Best let Jackie sleep on, she decided. That was the best remedy she knew for all sorts of ills. Then the large blue eyes were open, and Jackie blinked as a shaft of sunlight filtered into the bedroom.

'Oh. I . . . I brought coffee,' said Janet, 'but I'll leave it till later for you.

Just go back to sleep, dear.'

'No, pull the curtains, Mother, please. Sleeping late gives me a headache. I'll be glad of the coffee, though.'

Janet sat down on a pretty chintz-covered bedroom chair and stared at her daughter.

'Feel better now, after a sleep?'

'Yes,' lied Jackie.

She watched her mother get up and cross to the window, a sure sign that she was rather nervous and wanted to say something.

'Darling, about Jon . . . '

'Look, Mummy, it's a long story. And it isn't all about Jonathan, though he comes into it. Just let me get up and begin to feel alive again, and I'll tell you all about it. Okay?'

'Okay,' said Janet, smiling with relief.

Whatever it was, Jackie was not going to shut her out. With her usual brisk step, she went out of the bedroom and down to the kitchen, while Jackie sat up and sipped her coffee, then sighed as she swung her long slim legs out of bed. It was no use hiding in bed.

Downstairs, over part of the breakfast that Janet had cooked, Jackie told her mother all about the Naismiths, skipping a little over her own friendship with Adrian. Her mother's eyes had grown more round until she came to what was found in the attic.

'Tom Dennison probably didn't tell us everything,' she said in reply to her mother's question, 'but it looks as though there had been quite a small gang involved in counterfeit money. The Naismiths were involved, also Cynthia's father, Freddy Clarke, who got arrested when the notes were found in his possession.

'The Naismiths had a small printing business, so Mrs Naismith, who had managed to book a week at their usual holiday house being an off-peak time, took the plates with her and hid them. She thought they would never be connected with the house at Goodrington, especially with other people living there, and all she had to do to get them back was to re-book for another holiday.'

Jackie was quiet for a moment, remembering her own surprise when Tom had told them about Mrs Naismith.

'So Adrian's mother is alive after all,' she said. 'Is she still in Liverpool?'

Tom shook his head.

'No, I'm afraid she's dead. Her heart wasn't good, and the upset had been too much for her. No, Derek Naismith's grief for his wife was quite genuine.'

Hetty had glanced at Maude, exchanging a look of sympathy. Their sympathy for Derek Naismith returned, and Maude sighed a little. Perhaps it had not all been lies . . .

'They aren't the most accomplished of crooks,' Tom said, with a wry smile. 'Cynthia has more ability, perhaps, but they were poor at working out the best way to get into your attic without arousing suspicion. Unfortunately for them, Jackie arrived to stay . . . and locked the door.'

'It must have been frustrating for them,' said Jackie, as she remembered.

'Frustrating,' said Janet.

'Yes — three women, always in and out. I didn't even have a studio upstairs, and when I think of the hours I made Adrian sit still for his portrait, when he must have wanted to go racing up to that attic! Even Cynthia had a go at a 'girls together' act, but I always felt that she didn't really like me. Now I see it couldn't have been pleasant for her to watch her husband take out another girl. She must have had to keep reminding herself that it was necessary, in order to try to recover the plates. No wonder she hung around on the fringe!'

'Well, I hope we never hear of them again,' said Janet, 'and it's lovely to have you home.'

Jackie's hair dropped along her cheek.

'I . . . I may not be home for long, Mother. As a matter of fact, I . . . I thought I would like to go back to

London, and try to get some commercial work. I feel rather aimless here.'

Janet turned away and began to stack breakfast things on the draining board.

'I had hoped you and Jonathan Nelson would make a go of it,' she said bluntly.

'Mother!' cried Jackie, 'there was never any question . . . '

'My dear . . . ' Janet turned round purposefully, 'I've worried about that a great deal. Sometimes I've felt it was my fault if it didn't turn out that way. I . . . I rather criticised Jonathan because I felt he was being selfish at his parents' expense. Well, I was wrong, Jackie. Very wrong. And it serves me right as it would have been none of my business anyway. My . . . my only excuse is that one tends to look from all angles at young men who start to hang around one's daughter.'

'It was nothing to do with what you said, or how you felt,' said Jackie, then she flushed guiltily, knowing that was not quite true. She *had* passed on that criticism to Jonathan and it had been one more wedge between them.

Yet how could she tell her mother about the shock and contempt on Jonathan's face when he found Adrian in her bedroom, and how he had not even waited to hear her explanation, or to help her when she needed him most.

'I went over to Merton Lodge last week, and it all looks wonderful,' Janet was saying. 'Brigadier Nelson is totally won over, and he's usually such a stick-in-the-mud over some things, and hates change. But Jonathan insisted on having the Lodge put into first-class condition *now*, when it most needs it, otherwise he said it would be a ruin by the time it was his responsibility. And what's more, Jackie, Jonathan paid for it all himself. He's got his uncle's money, you see. Evelyn told me.'

'Oh, Mother! I don't want to hear. What a couple of old gossips you and Mrs Nelson are.'

'Jackie!'

Janet was very offended.

'I'm sorry, Mother, but all this is Jonathan's affair, not ours.'

How she wished she had remembered that before, she thought dismally, remembering how his face had hardened. She should never have made such comments about him.

'That girl has gone, too,' Janet told her.

'What girl?' Janet tried to appear indifferent.

'That Miss Hodge. We met her in Jonathan's company in Bristol. Remember?'

She nodded.

'She's gone to London, and Evelyn says Jonathan hopes to start his own firm when he feels he has enough experience.'

'I can only wish him luck,' said Jackie rather wearily.

She hoped she would not run into Janetta Hodge in London, then she smiled wryly. London wasn't quite the same as Chipping Sodbury.

'Oh, and Mrs Charles at Willowdale

wants to see you. She saw your picture at the Lodge and wondered if you could do a painting of Willowdale for Linda. You remember Linda? She married a Canadian and is living in Ottawa. Mrs Charles is flying out there next spring and thought it would make a nice gift for her to take.'

Jackie brightened at the prospect of some work.

'I'll get changed and go now,' she decided. 'Willowdale is quite an interesting old Georgian house, and there's a good view from the bottom of the drive. Did Mrs Charles say to come any time?'

'Any time,' said Janet, relieved.

It was good to see Jackie with some life in her again.

★   ★   ★

It was delightful to be painting Willowdale, thought Jackie, as she caught the riotous colour of the clematis which clung to the walls,

270

mingling in with New Dawn roses, now fading a little. She had caught the house at a slightly oblique angle which gave it an air of dignity and elegance, and a sort of understated beauty which made one wonder about it, and long to explore.

'It's good, very good, Jackie!'

She jumped, startled. Cars often passed by while she was working, but she had learned to disregard them, only one had stopped a short distance away and now Jonathan was standing behind her.

'Your mother told me where to find you. I always seem to choose a time when you're out!'

'Did you want to see me specially?' she croaked.

The unexpected sight of him had set her heart racing, and her mouth felt dry, even as she turned to look at him. He looked older, and the laughing teasing look in his eyes had gone.

'Yes.'

He nodded and after a moment she

began to wipe her brushes. She would do no more useful work on the picture today. Already her hand was shaking, though she managed to pack her tubes of paint into a wooden box, then wipe her fingers on a rag soaked in spirit.

'Sorry about the smell,' she said, as casually as she could.

'I like it.'

'I'll walk back along home and put my things away, then you can tell me how ... how I can help you. Is it another commission?'

He looked at her consideringly.

'No.'

'Oh.' She felt rather disappointed. Willowdale would soon be finished, then she would be back to considering what to do next.

'Can't you put them in the back of the car?'

'It isn't far, and my hands are dirty.'

'So's your face. You've got paint all across your forehead. For goodness' sake, Jackie, what does it matter? Get in.'

Nerves made his voice sound snappy, and without a word she put her picture flat out on the back of the car seat, and her equipment in the boot. Of course it would not matter to Jonathan what she looked like. He was hardly likely to be interested now.

He got in and they drove off at a lick.

'When you give me a lift home, why do you always hare off in the wrong direction?' she asked. 'Where are you taking me this time?'

She was very conscious of the paint on her face.

'Don't worry, I'm not abducting you,' he told her, and the colour ran into her cheeks.

'I'd hardly imagine that you were!'

He drove to a quiet spot, a place where they had once gone on a picnic, a very long time ago. It seemed like another age, in fact, as he stopped the car and they both sat staring round. Jonathan seemed to be lost in thought, and Jackie felt hot and sticky, and even more conscious of the smell of turpentine clinging to her fingers, and the streak of paint on her face.

'What do you want to see me about?' she asked evenly.

'Moths always go to the candle,' he told her. 'Odd, isn't it?'

'You don't want to see me?'

'No. But I can't help myself.'

She sat still, trying to put this into perspective.

'I knew you were still at home. Your mother mentioned it when she talked with my mother on the telephone only yesterday. But I find you interfering with my work and I don't want to risk designing a building with the roof likely to collapse!'

She managed a smile.

'I'd hate to be responsible for that. It's all right, though, Jonathan. I'm going to London soon. I'll be well out of your orbit then.'

He turned to look at her.

'I'd got high hopes when I saw that picture.'

'What picture?'

'The one you're doing now. It's got depth and feeling to it. I thought for a moment that you might have put a bit of yourself into it.'

'I . . . I don't know what you mean.'

'I know you don't, more's the pity.' He reached out and pulled at a leafy branch close to the side of the car.

'Haven't you ever really cared about anybody, Jackie? So much that you feel like murdering someone if they even dare to look at them? So much that you could even be jealous of the cat for sitting in their lap?'

Again she wanted to laugh, but she knew it was not really meant to be funny. She thought of her own jealousy of Janetta Hodge, whom she had not even got to know. Yet just because she was in Jonathan's company, and she knew he was taking her out, she had felt she hated the girl. Yet she might have liked her, if they had met under normal circumstances, such as in a friend's house, or at College. She had actually hated an unknown girl!

'Yes,' she said huskily, 'I've felt like that.'

'Then can't you understand in the very least how I felt when I saw Adrian Naismith in your bedroom? *And* saying you'd invited him there! Don't forget, we didn't know at that time that he really was a crook. We only suspected that something was wrong. And you'd painted his portrait, *and* you'd let him kiss you! Oh yes, I saw you when he brought you home one evening, and I felt like killing him then.'

Jonathan sighed.

'In fact, I tried very hard to be fair to the man, feeling that my distrust of him could be caused mainly by jealousy. No one could deny he's very good-looking, could they?'

'No,' she agreed.

She was trying to sort out her thoughts and emotions, which seemed to alternate between wild soaring hope, then the sickness of depression. He couldn't be blamed for walking out on her, but did he still blame her for the low opinion of him she had expressed so freely?

'I . . . I'm sorry I said what I did . . . about . . . being selfish to your parents. We . . . I know now that it was untrue.'

His lip curled.

'No need to apologise. I allow people to think what they like. I've only got myself to live with, and I find it easier if I can respect myself, too. I suppose that's why I've been finding things hard going recently.'

'It's all right,' she said quickly. 'I understand, about Adrian. It's forgotten . . . '

'Because you've found out I'm not such a selfish villain as you believed!'

The words were light, but she could feel the tension in him as he waited for her answer. Jackie forgot about the paint on her forehead and her sticky fingers.

'No. I understand because I felt like that, too. Only about Janetta Hodge. I don't even know her, but I felt I could scratch her eyes out!'

'Janetta! But . . . but she was just a colleague of mine.'

'Whom you took out in the evenings.'

'Yes, but . . . ' Understanding began to dawn. 'You were jealous of her?'

Jackie nodded, the telltale colour in her cheeks again. 'Yes.'

He threw away the crumpled leaf and drew her into his arms.

'Why didn't you give me some sort of hint before? Why keep me at arm's length when you knew how much I loved you?'

'I didn't! You never said you did.'

'I told you I did years ago, when I was about sixteen. You were always my girl. You know that. I even asked you to marry me.'

'I thought your parents had talked you into it.'

Jonathan laughed, holding her close.

'Oh, Jackie darling, what an idiot you are! How could you think such a thing? I thought you were just using that as an excuse . . . '

'Now who's the idiot? You were just as bad.'

He kissed her, then kissed her again, and any doubt she'd ever had of their love for one another was removed for all time.

'And you believe me now?' he asked.

'Anyone who can kiss paint off a girl's forehead must be genuine. I'm a mess, darling.'

'You're just as I love you. I say, what will your mother think?'

'Oh, she'll be pleased,' Jackie told him, with conviction.

'And your aunts?'

'They'll have a wonderful time, buying new clothes for our wedding. Oh, goodness!'

'What?'

'You haven't asked me to marry you again.'

'Do I have to go through all that?'

'Yes, and properly this time.'

Janet glanced at the clock. Jackie was very late in coming home for a meal, and she wondered, sometimes hopefully, if Jonathan and she were putting things right between them. Any fool could see they were eating their hearts out for one another.

The telephone rang and it was Evelyn Nelson. Even as they talked, Jonathan's car rolled up and Janet watched with interest while the two young people got out, and walked in the gate. The sun had long since disappeared for the day, but it still seemed to shine on their young faces.

'Evelyn,' said Janet, 'I'll have to ring you back. The children are at the door. And Evelyn, don't go out, will you? If you ask me, they have some news for us!'

THE END

We do hope that you have enjoyed reading this large print book.

Did you know that all of our titles are available for purchase?

We publish a wide range of high quality large print books including:
Romances, Mysteries, Classics
General Fiction
Non Fiction and Westerns

Special interest titles available in large print are:
The Little Oxford Dictionary
Music Book, Song Book
Hymn Book, Service Book

Also available from us courtesy of Oxford University Press:
Young Readers' Dictionary
(large print edition)
Young Readers' Thesaurus
(large print edition)

For further information or a free brochure, please contact us at:
Ulverscroft Large Print Books Ltd.,
The Green, Bradgate Road, Anstey,
Leicester, LE7 7FU, England.
Tel: (00 44) **0116 236 4325**
Fax: (00 44) **0116 234 0205**

CAVE OF FIRE

Rebecca King

Lost in a South American rain forest with sexy Nick Devlin, Dany knew she was a million miles away from the safe world represented by her fiancé, Marcus. Only goodness knew how she would be able to return to that world — for to return was one thing; to forget was another . . .